You Don't Know What I Have Done

By Sheila McNaughton

Published By
Breaking Rules Publishing

Soft Cover – 10087
Published by Breaking Rules Publishing
St Petersburg, Florida
www.breakingrulespublishing.com

Acknowledgment

This book is dedicated to my sister, Sharon Flanagan and to the memory of our mom, Bridget Mary Bayes.

Thank you to my writing pals, Jan Golden and Sheila Wasserman. Our regular get togethers have kept me motivated and on track. A special thanks to John Trese, Firefighter/EMT for the City of Largo, FL. My editor, Mark Mathes, has been incredible. His knowledge and assistance helped me become a better writer and create a more entertaining story. I appreciate the continued support from my family and friends.

All of this is easier because of the encouragement, help and unceasing love from my husband, John.

Alzheimer's is a difficult disease for the patient, loved ones and caregivers. For more information and resources please visit www.alz.org.

Chapter 1

Ashes and bits of bone were in the oaken urn decorated with a single gold shamrock. It sat atop the green silk draped table, next to her picture in front of the altar of St Mary's Catholic Church. She wouldn't have liked that photo, never wanted her picture to be taken, always hated how she looked. Said her hair was messy, her glasses were crooked or the background wasn't right. Something was always wrong. In truth, she feared they would see the photo and find her. Find her and take her away for what she had done.

In the front pew stood her three children and their spouses. The oldest, Ian, next to his wife Rose. Close but not touching. In the middle, as was her place in the birth order stood Lizzie and her husband Dan, their arms and hands intertwined, leaning into each other. Next was the youngest son, Kevin with his wife Becca, his arm bent at the elbow was tight behind his back to prevent any accidental touching. Grandchildren, their spouses and great grandchildren, all forty-nine of them ranging in age from ten months to thirty-five years old, stood in the next rows of pews.

Margaret Mary Murphy was eighty-five years old when she died. Maggie, as she was known and her husband, Sam, had been members of this community for over 30 years. They moved to St Pete Beach after Sam retired as an executive from

Goodyear Tire and Rubber Company in Akron, Ohio. "Akron is the rubber capitol of the world," he used to say with a sly grin and a wink when asked about his work. They wanted to be near their three children and the grandkids but also to revel in the year round sunny days and warm gulf waters. Six months ago Sam died suddenly. Heart attack at ninety-one.

A determined Irish Catholic, Maggie attended daily mass whenever possible. Sam went with her, not from a devotion to God, but a powerful love of Maggie. He was her protector and champion. "The love of my live and my reason for being," is how each described the other. They loved their kids and the Gee-kids as Sam took to calling the passel of grandchildren but no one ever came between Sam and Maggie.

They were the perfect grandparents. With a cooler filled with sodas and sandwiches, piles of towels and toys for the sand they bundled the grandkids into their white SUV and headed for the beach. Any beach would do, though they favored the uncivilized beauty of Fort DeSoto at the southern end of Pinellas County. The Gee-kids, no matter their ages, never tired of spending time with Grandpa Sam and Grand Maggie. They ferried kids to school and scouts and sporting events. They stayed through all the games and could be heard loudly cheering on the team or spied quietly offering a hug and words of support to a young player. It could have been one of theirs or anyone's child. "Everyone needs more people and more love in their lives," Sam would say in his deep comforting voice.

Both of them dressed in matching costumes for Halloween and accompanied the little ones out trick or treating. Sam was the prisoner with a ball and chain around his ankle while Maggie played the cop keeping him in line. They were hobos one year, hippies the next and to everyone amazement, Maggie as Tinkerbelle and Sam as Peter Pan the following year. They spent days trying to find green tights large enough for Sam. At six foot four, nothing fit him so they dyed a pair of old beige long johns a fetching shade of emerald green then Maggie made the rest of the outfit including the dashing hat complete with feather. Sam was the hit of the neighborhood as he walked around singing, "I'll never grow up. I'll never grow, not me."

Sam played Santa right up through his last Christmas. All but the littlest ones knew it was Grandpa Sam but that did not dispel the magic of the moment when he walked through the front door and bellowed, "Ho, Ho, Ho. Where are those good little girls and boys?"

Maggie and Sam were mainstays at the annual Church Holiday Bazaar. They helped set up the tables for the crafters to display and sell their handmade ornaments, knitted booties, festive door wreaths or any number of delightful treasures. Folks waited in line an hour before the doors opened on sale day. Maggie always made peanut butter and chocolate chip cookies and the best ever double chocolate cake for the Holiday Sweet Shop. Sam's favorite task was sorting through the donated stuff for the White Elephant Sale. All manner of odds and ends were brought in to sell to raise money for the children's programs at the church. Old manual typewriters, fancy china, serving dishes, books and a wide variety of household goods. People brought in the strangest objects in hopes of confounding Sam about its original purpose but he either figured out what it actually was or made up a fantastic story about the piece. He worked the room on sale day. "You know you can't live without that beautiful platter. Think of how impressed your family will be when you come to the table to present the roast beef, potatoes and tender carrots for Sunday dinner." He made the sale. Five more dollars for the kids.

They had their own special table at Wednesday night Bingo. Maggie and Sam got there early to visit with friends, have dinner and play a few hands of euchre before the bingo games began. Women outnumbered the men by three to one, easily. Sam became the unofficial guardian of the unaccompanied women. He made sure they got to their cars safely or if someone needed a ride Sam would arrange for a couple who lived nearby to play chauffer. The women delighted in Sam but knew he belonged to Maggie.

Maggie had been officially diagnosed with Alzheimer's three years ago though she had known for some time before the terrible disease was robbing her of her memories and her current life. Sam knew too, but together they decided not to tell the children. Two weeks before his sudden death Sam confided in Phyllis, Maggie's best friend, who was sworn to secrecy. The children found out a few months ago. She managed to fool most people into believing she was fine. Verbal and visual cues let her know what was expected. If those around her welcomed a newcomer with a smile and a hug, she did too. If people laughed when watching a movie or TV show, she laughed. She adapted to her surroundings and kept quiet.

Car rides were always one of Maggie's pleasures. As long as there was a vehicle available she knew she could go anywhere, do anything. After morning Mass, she and Sam would head off to the park or the beach. Maggie kept a bag packed in the trunk with towels, blanket, sun screen and a couple of books. She even had small overnight bags with extra clothes and necessities in case they were invited to stay with friends for a weekend. Always be prepared for adventures were her mantra.

After Sam died she began asking one of her children to pick her up for Mass, dinner or a visit. No excuse given and no questions asked. They all knew her reflexes where not what they had been. Her cataract surgery three years earlier made night driving more difficult. After all, she was in her eighties.

The loss of Sam forced a major change in the lives of their children. And now, Maggie's death left them drifting and uncertain. Their parents were part of the ebb and flow of their lives but now they realized they were in fact a defining force.

The mass was short but the eulogy long. Father Mike had known the Murphys since they moved to town. It had been his sad duty to officiate at Sam's funeral and now, so soon after, it was Maggie's.

Tall white candles flickered on the marble altar behind him as he said, "We all know of Maggie's devotion to the Church. She was particularly close to St. Jude, the patron saint of lost causes. Everyone, at one time or another has heard Maggie say, 'If St. Jude can help me, and I know what a lost cause I am, he can help you. Say a little prayer and I know he'll be listening.' I once asked about her lost cause. She only smiled sadly and said it was enough to keep poor St. Jude busy for years and years." He pointed upward and said, "I don't believe there is anything to stop Margaret Mary Murphy from entering heaven this day."

Some of Maggie's friends wanted to speak. Phyllis walked slowly with a cane to the front of the church. Her hands shook slightly as she touched a hankie to her wet eyes, but her voice was clear. "Maggie has been my friend for almost thirty years. I never had a sister. Neither did Maggie, not really. She and I met when we were in our fifties and became best friends right away. Maggie has been my rock and my bingo buddy all these years. I do not think about her last months but the wonderful happy years before."

Holding tight to her hankie and the podium, Phyllis looked out over the crowd. "Maggie was there for me when my husband Bill died ten years ago. It was a freak accident, a fall from a stepladder in the back yard of our son's home hitting his head on a tree root, putting him in a coma." She looked down at her shaking hand holding the microphone then back up to look at Lizzie. "Sam was good, too, but it was Maggie who came at the first call and stayed with me to the end of Bill's life. After he was gone she was there at the house for days, helping me, helping everyone through the process. And, when my kids went home to get back to their lives Maggie was there. Calling every day, stopping by. Allowing me to grieve but not allowing me to disappear from the world. She kept me alive and helped me to live. I miss Maggie, my friend, my sister."

Father Mike stood at the alter looking out at the group assembled on this sad day and was not surprised at what he saw. With a weak smile he said, "When someone of Maggie's age dies you expect to see only family and a few friends. This is not the case for Maggie. Even the friends of Maggie's grandchildren are here to show their love and respect."

Sweeping his eyes over the faces of her children he continued, "Maggie or Grand Maggie as she was called was always available for her children, her grandchildren, great grandchildren and their friends. I remember seeing Maggie sitting by the pool at Lizzie and Dan's house talking to one tearful teenage girl, a friend of one of the Gee-kids, after her heart had been broken by some loutish boy. By the time Maggie was done that young girl was sitting tall in her chair and taking animatedly about her plans for the future. Maggie encouraged their dreams. She defended the parents in a way the kids understood. I have to say, many a wise and kind word from Maggie kept those kids on the right path. I see some of you today that owe your success, in part, to Maggie Murphy."

Ian stood up, tall like his dad but with a bit more bulk, he walked quickly to the podium. He turned to look at his wife, Rose, whose eyes and nose were wet and red, twisting a sodden tissue in her lap. She was a beautiful woman and he was lucky she had stayed with him all these years. They sat up late last night drinking decaf coffee from mugs that read "Coffee & You! That's All I Need". They had been a gift from Maggie when their marriage was going through a rough patch. Laughing and crying they remembered this amazing woman.

"Mom's faith helped her through the dark times, the death of her family in Ireland when she was young, the horrors of living alone in London during the war, the struggles she encountered in America as a young war bride and losing the love of her life, my Dad, my Sam, as she always called him. Mom celebrated all the milestones of our family with flair and passion."

Running his hand through his hair, he faltered then looked to his wife. Shaking his head from side to side he said, "Mom never missed a birthday or an anniversary. It wasn't the money or the gift she gave that meant the most, it was the letter that accompanied it. Hand written in her beautiful script on fine ivory stationary. It was a tribute to you on your day. A reminder of how important you were to her and the family. I've kept every letter from her. I went through the box last night. I want to share part of one of her letters with you today."

Ian looked at Rose who nodded her head and tried to smile. "My darling Ian," he read. "Today you are twenty-one. A man, though in my eyes if you live to be a hundred, you will always be my sweet little boy. I hope you don't mind. I see the strong man you have become and know you have the potential to be so much more. You have your Daddy's sense of business and will do well out in the world of money. You have the Irish love of a good time so you must watch out. Be careful not to wallow in it. Most importantly, you have a kind and tender heart. No man likes to hear it but it is necessary for you to know it and nurture that part of yourself. That kind heart will bring you more happiness than any job or paycheck ever will." He stopped reading, paused and slowly raised his eyes. "She went on to share more with me but you get the point. She was straightforward and loving. I kept that one page letter with me, folded up in my wallet, all these years. When I found myself confused or dumbfounded with life I would read it." Ian stopped, took a deep breath and in a voice husky with unshed tears he said, "Our family meant everything to her; family was the most important thing in her life." It was all he managed to say before the tears fell. Father Mike took the microphone and motioned to Kevin to step forward.

Tall and thin, like his Dad, Kevin ambled to the front of the church. He was the joker in the family, the salesman with the cocky smile and quick wit. Kevin brought laughter to the crowd when he talked about Maggie's fanatical desire for cleanliness. "Neat and tidy. Everything in its place and a place for everything. Cleanliness is next to Godliness. All the clichés fit. No matter what was going on with the Murphy family, that house was cleaned thoroughly every week. All of us kids involved in washing windows, laundry, sweeping, dusting and cooking. I am a natural born slob, not sure where that came from, but that's the way it is." Laughing slightly he looked from Lizzie to Ian who were both nodding their heads and smiling as silent tears ran down their cheeks.

"A headache to Mom and then my poor wife Becca. But no matter my nature it wasn't possible in the Murphy household. I was the only kid on the block made to wash his bike at least once a week. No mud on my tires. No dirt caked under the seat from bringing my bike to a sliding stop in the empty lot down the street." He hesitated, and then eyes bright with tears, said, "Mom and Dad taught us respect for our surroundings which spilled over into respecting others and ourselves. Those lessons stayed with me and are part of the reason I have success in my life today."

His face reddened as he looked out over the crowd of people. Maggie might not have been proud of him this day for she had known his success was in business only, not with his family. His kids were barely talking to him, and his wife, well he didn't even look her in the eye these days. He stepped down from the alter and saw his sister shiver and snuggle into Dan's body for support. He and Becca had never shared such a natural, comfortable connection to each other.

A thin, good looking woman in her early fifties, smartly dressed in a black suit with long blonde hair held in a loose bun at the nape of her neck, walked confidently to the front of the church and reached out for the microphone. Large gold hoops at her ears and wrists glinted in the sunlight as she turned to face the mourners. "My name is Georgia Walden. Lizzie and I were friends in high school and beyond. I am one of those kids Father Mike talked about. I had a lot of rough stuff to deal with growing up. None of it worth mentioning now," she said as she slowly shook her head from side to side. "I'm not sure where I was headed back then but it wasn't a good place. Then I met Lizzie and her family. I'll never forget the day I met Maggie. She took one look at me, handed me a glass of ice tea and said 'Everything's going to be okay.'"

Georgia grasped hold of the podium a bit tighter. "I don't know how she knew things were bad. I hadn't said much to Lizzie. I didn't want to scare her away. But, Maggie knew, somehow. Later that first evening, she took me aside and said nothing that happened to me had anything to do with me or my future. She said every day I decide what kind of day I'm going to have." Looking down and blinking slowly the tears dropped on to her cheeks. Raising her head and glancing towards Lizzie she said, "I decide. That was a new concept for me. She told me be prepared for a fantastic day, every day. Wake up and feel good. Find wonderful people to be with, fun stuff to do. Learn something interesting and exciting every day. Do not take a single day for granted. Each one is a blessing and a miracle. Now I can't say I got all that and followed it right away but over the four years of high school, I saw what Maggie was talking about. She lived each day to the fullest."

Georgia paused to look down at the table with the urn and photo then raised her eyes and said loudly, "Maggie celebrated the smallest joys right along with the biggest triumphs. She showed me how to live a happy life. By the time I graduated I was an honor student with straight A's and a full scholarship to Florida State University." She straightened her shoulders and stood just a bit taller. "Today I'm happily married to a kind, loving man named Dean. I have a son and a daughter. I'll soon be a grandma. I teach music to middle school children. I try to teach them the lessons Maggie taught me. Live every day as if it were your last. Treasure the moments."

She turned to hand the microphone to Father Mike then stopped. "We were all blessed to have Maggie in our lives," she said and her eyes rose to the heavens.

Lizzie was the last to speak. Tall and slender, the black knee length fitted dress was at odds with the long, wild mahogany hair and the large multicolor dangling earrings and bracelets she wore. She'd tried to find something less flashy in her jewelry box but then remembered her mom saying some years ago, "Oh Lizzie, you know you love the gaudy stuff and you wear it so well. You could even wear it to a funeral and look ravishing."

She took the time walking to the microphone to compose herself. "Thank you all for coming here today. Mom would be happy to see each of you. She did so love a gathering of family and friends, no matter the reason. My Mom taught me all the right things to do to run a house but more importantly, all the loving things to do to make it a home."

Lizzie paused and looked at Dan. He was smiling and mouthed, "I love you."

"Mom knew how to read your heart's desire. When I was in second grade I wanted to be, had to be, a witch for Halloween. Money was tight but she found enough to buy the pattern and black and orange cotton fabric. She sewed the long dress with large bat like sleeves and constructed a tall pointed witch's hat. She stayed up long past midnight to finish the costume. For an extra touch she made a small stuffed orange pumpkin on a strap to be worn across my shoulder like a purse. There were enough scraps left over to piece together a tote bag to hold all the candy I would collect that night." She paused. "My mom was magical."

Lizzie took in the crowd sitting in the hard wooden pews of the massive stone church. She saw the sad faces of the people she knew and loved and those who shared bits of her life like T.J. sitting in the back. There were total strangers; the grey haired man in the dark suit and red tie sitting beside a small elegant woman in a dark dress softly daubing at her eyes with a white hankie and in front of them four older grey haired women in matching bright yellow tops. She had more to say but her voice faltered. Her breathing became shallow, her eyes misted over. She had to stop now or risk saying the one thing only she and Dan knew. Maggie was a murderer.

Chapter 2

Five Months Earlier

It was Saturday three weeks after her dad died. The sun was brilliant hot, almost 90 degrees. Lizzie had the convertible top down and the AC blasting on her little red Miata two-seater sports car. It had been a fiftieth birthday present from Dan. Not practical for her job as a Realtor or grandchildren. A fun car, just because he loved her and knew she would enjoy every minute behind the wheel. She was listening to Bob Dylan sing *Sara.* Lizzie loved that song, the tribute to his wife always touched her heart. It didn't matter that Bob Dylan and his wife Sara had been divorced for over 30 years. At the time he wrote it, as he sang it, he knew her and loved her. She smiled and sang along softly with the words: "Sweet love of my life. Sara. Sara. Radiant jewel, mystical wife."

The afternoon traffic was worse than normal. A semi with a wide load was slowly moving west on Walsingham in the right lane. The left lane was blocked by a SUV going maybe 20 miles an hour. A few horns honked which seemed to make the driver go even slower. Finally the truck pulled off into the parking lot of a plaza and angry motorists blasted past the slow moving vehicle.

Lizzie was trying not to be upset as she said aloud, "Why do these old people get out and drive during busy times." She swerved into the right lane and prepared to speed past the car with the elderly driver. One quick glance to her left and Lizzie almost lost control of her car. "Mom?" She could see her mother, eyes straight ahead, tissues sticking up around fingers tightly grasping the steering wheel, her head bobbing and her mouth moving as if in prayer.

"Mom, Mom, what are you doing?" Lizzie yelled, her voice lost in the traffic noise. "Shit. What am I going to do?" She reached for her purse on the passenger seat and rooted around for the cell phone. She stopped before hitting five, her mom's speed dial number. The ringing phone would only panic her. Maggie was barely able to use the cell phone when she was not in distress.

Traffic continued to move at above the posted forty miles per hour. Maybe Mom got off the road Lizzie thought. Making a U-turn at the next light she headed back the way she came. No blue police lights were visible and still traffic was moving along. Now she was the one driving slowly as she gripped the steering wheel, her hands sweaty from the heat and fear, and leaned to the right looking in parking lots and side streets. "Mom, where are you?"

"She's okay. She has to be," Lizzie said as she made another U-turn at the light where she first saw her mother. She couldn't see anything from the right side of the road so at the next light she made another U-turn and drove east. One more drive around then I'll head to her condo she thought. A few blocks down just off the main road in the parking lot of the small fruit stand she saw her mom, dressed in white Capri pants and a red and white striped top standing beside the open driver's door. Lizzie hit the brakes and made a quick right turn on to the side street. Barely putting it in park, she jumped out and ran to her mother. "Mom, is everything alright?"

Maggie was startled when Lizzie raced around the rear of the vehicle calling to her. "Well of course. Stop yelling. People will hear you. I was a bit confused and that nice young girl, that nurse, called you and here you are," Maggie said in a loud whisper.

"What nurse? I saw you on the road. Cars were backed up behind you and the truck; you couldn't have been going more than twenty miles an hour. Something could've happened to you." Lizzie's voice was brittle as she reached out to hug her mom. Maggie's clothes were damp with sweat and her usually neat hair was plastered to her forehead.

"I'm fine. Don't be silly. I just had a bit of trouble finding the hospital. I have an appointment today," Maggie said patting her hair with her right hand. "I don't want to be late."

"What appointment? You don't have an appointment and the hospital is not on this road," Lizzie said aware of the flush on her mom's face.

"Of course it is. It is somewhere down there," she pointed towards town, away from the beaches. "On the left side, isn't it? I can't imagine why I can't find it. I just needed to go a few blocks more but I'm not sure what happened. The next thing I know that nice young girl was at the door and said she would call you. And here you are. Everything's fine, so don't make a scene."

"No one called me, Mom. I've been driving Walsingham Road looking for you. Listen it's hot out..."

"The nurse called you," Maggie said standing straighter and glaring at Lizzie. "I stopped the car. She came to the door and said she would help. I gave her my purse so she could find my phone and call you."

"You gave her your purse? Why did you give her your purse?" Lizzie demanded, waving her arm about.

Maggie cocked her head to the left and right as if looking for someone. "She'll be right back. She...she went to the gas station over there to get me some water. I told her no, I'm fine but she went anyway. It is terribly hot today."

Lizzie looked around the plaza. Right in front of her was a permanent fruit and vegetable stand with bottles of water in a large blue plastic barrel. The sign read Ice Cold Water $1.00 a Bottle. At the corner of Walsingham was a Hess gas station now empty of cars. Maybe she was on her way back but somehow Lizzie doubted it.

"Mom, I don't know where the woman is but we need to get you home."

"Well, we can't just drive off without saying thank you. We can wait for a few minutes, until she gets back. Nice woman, nurse, worked at the hospital I go to. I'm feeling much better now that you're here dear. You can follow me home as soon as we thank her. I want to give her some money." Maggie opened the purse and found her wallet.

"Oh my Lord," cried Maggie. "I thought I had money in my wallet. I had won the jackpot at Bingo on Friday. It was a lot of money. I don't remember how much. I was going to go to the bank on Saturday but I don't know why I didn't. Maybe it's at home. Maybe I left it on the table. Did I go to the bank on Saturday?" Maggie's head was bent as she combed through the jumbled mess in her purse, pulling out a notebook, lipstick, tissues and compact, throwing them on the driver's seat.

"Here," she said loudly as she pulled a thick white envelope out. "Oh Thank God, this is it." The flap of the envelope opened and dozens of neatly clipped coupons fluttered in the air and fell to the ground. "Oh no. No. It's not the money. No. I must have gone to the bank. But where is the receipt?"

"It's okay. Today is Saturday. Maybe you went to the bank."

"It's not okay. Where's the money? Did I go to the bank? Where's the receipt? Did you see it? Did I drop it?" Her face twisted in pain, eyes darting from the purse to the ground, Maggie cried out, "It must have blown out of my purse under the car." She grabbed hold of the door and started to lower herself to her knees.

"Mom. Stop that. It's not on the ground. Those are just coupons." Lizzie grabbed Maggie by the arm. "Stop it."

"Then you look. It's a lot of money and if I don't have the receipt...what did I do with the money? It could be on the ground. You look now," yelled Maggie pushing Lizzie to the ground.

"Alright. Alright." Exasperated, Lizzie got down on her hands and knees on the dirty cracked asphalt to look under the car. "Nothing but pavement and coupons. Honestly."

"Keep looking. Pick them up. One of them must be the receipt. What'll I do?" cried Maggie, sounding like the heroine in need of rescuing in an old black and white movie. "What'll I do?" she continued to repeat softly, her fingers worrying the gold cross she wore around her neck.

Down on her knees Lizzie dutifully picked up the loose coupons. She followed Maggie's pointing fingers and chased after a few that floated onto the asphalt of the adjacent parking lot. She stopped short of going out into the street for fifty cents off a box of cereal.

"That's it Mom. We got them all, Lizzie said as she wiped the pebbles from her knees. "No bank receipt, just coupons. It'll be okay. We'll find the money or the receipt. Let's get you home. It's hot out here. We'll take my car. I'll have someone bring me back for yours later," Lizzie said as she helped her mom into the passenger seat. One last look around and Lizzie knew the nice woman was not coming back. Hopefully all she wanted was the quick money. At least she didn't take her credit cards, phone or keys. She didn't hurt her. Just money

After Lizzie raised the rag top and clicked the snaps to lock it in place she stared through the front windshield barely seeing anything around her. What just happened she thought? Ever since Daddy died Mom has been off but that was to be expected after all those years together. We need to spend more time with her. I have to talk to Dan and the boys. Lizzie stopped at the next light and turned to look closely at her mom.

A confident smiling Maggie said, "I'm so happy we get to spend some time together. What a lovely treat. I'm not sure what happened. I just sort of got lost. Nothing looked familiar.

I just wanted to get off the street. Then that nice girl was there. She was probably on her way to work. That's why she didn't come back. She saw you and knew I was fine. She's a nurse, you know, at the hospital where I go. I would love a cup of tea. Wouldn't you darling?"

"How do you know she was a nurse?"

"I told her I was going there and she said that's where she worked as a nurse. Wasn't that a delightful coincidence, dear?" said Maggie leaning back comfortably in the seat and wiping her forehead with a tissue.

* * *

At the condo, Maggie and Lizzie sat at the kitchen table with the afternoon sun coming through the large window, drinking their tea. Steam rose from the cups and the air smelled faintly of honey and chamomile. "I love this room. My Sam and I had breakfast here most mornings. Tea for me and coffee for my Sam. Bagels and fruit and the St Pete Times. What a lovely way to start the day. My Sam." She turned her head and stared out the window to the water. "My Sam," she repeated.

Lizzie was wishing for something stronger than tea. A little too early for that. She didn't want to broach the subject of the money or driving.

Before Lizzie could speak, Maggie said, "I was tired. My friend and I sat up talking about the old days after the others left last night. I shouldn't drive when I know I haven't had a good night's sleep. I'll be more careful. Sorry to have been a bother. I know you have things to do. Where is Dan today? Working?"

"No Mom, it's Saturday and he decided to play a round of golf with George and two guys from work. He rarely plays on Saturday. That's why I was out this afternoon. Doing a little shopping. Where were you going?" she asked tentatively.

"Just a drive. You know I love to drive," Maggie said with a sunny smile.

"But you said you had an appointment at the hospital."

"Why would I have an appointment on a Saturday? Don't be silly. What did you say Dan was doing?"

"Golf. Dan is golfing," Lizzie took a deep breath and said a bit too loudly, "Listen now, we need to talk about what happened today. About your driving."

"Listen? Really just who do you think you are? Listen? You listen. I can drive whenever and where ever I want. I won't be talked to like that," Maggie said gripping her cup tightly and watching the hot tea slosh in the cup.

"Take it easy. I didn't mean to upset you. I'm concerned about you. That woman could have hurt you. What if she had been a mean person?" Lizzie said eyeing her mom closely.

"I don't open the door for mean people. Really," a frustrated Maggie firmly stated. "I'm sure the money is here or at the bank. Not to worry." Then she turned to look at Lizzie and a slight smile came to her face. "Let's not argue. It's such a beautiful day. Would you like another cup of tea, darling?"

Not to worry, thought Lizzie. She picked up her nearly empty cup and looked around the room. Lizzie had made the curtains from fabric she and Maggie had picked out together in one of their now famous shopping scenes. Maggie wanted a change, something fun and Floridian. Everyone in the fabric store could hear the two of them howling with laughter as they tried to decide on a suitable fabric. Should the kitchen have big footed clowns with scarlet red hair? Sam was always joking about a red headed Irishman coming to claim his Maggie. Maybe the dancing tiara wearing pink pigs would be cute. Or, how about the green gators with wide open mouths and palm trees? In the end they settled on a soft lemon yellow trimmed in a lime green. The tropical fruits were used as accents on the tea towels, napkins and dishes. Lizzie even found an old lemon and lime salt and pepper shaker at a church rummage sale.

"I love this room too, Mom," Lizzie said aloud and to herself she said, I miss you Daddy.

What would she say to her brothers? This was such an odd thing to happen. Thoughts swirling, she looked closely at her mom and saw frailty for the first time. Of course she had wrinkles, she was in her eighties but now she saw the translucent tissue paper quality to her skin, the slight tremor in her hands when she picked up the tea cup and the wariness in her eyes was not there before. She did not want to admit the truth. She had always said if something ever happens to mom, not when, as if she would live forever. She said the same thing about her dad and yet he was gone. Not if, when.

She had to think. Talk about something else. "Yes, Mom, let me get us both another cup of tea. The church rummage sale is coming up soon."

Chapter 3

Lizzie tossed her oversize brown leather tote bag and keys on the granite kitchen counter. The air in the condo felt funny. It was oddly quiet. "Mom? Where are you?"

A delicate rustle was all she could hear. Mom must have left a window open thought Lizzie as she headed down the hall. Once more she called out to her mom but heard nothing but a slight muffled noise. The door to the second bedroom was open to a tropical oasis of wicker furniture and soft greens and pinks. Lizzie took two steps into the room. Everything looked fine. She heard the noise again.

"Where are you?" she said as she hurried out the room and down the hall to the master bedroom. The sliding glass door was opened slightly to the balcony and the strong Gulf breeze was blowing the sheer drapes

Lizzie spun around as she heard the noise again. "Mom!" Lizzie yelled as she saw Maggie curled on her side on the floor of the large walk-in closet reaching, reaching for something Lizzie could not see. There was blood clinging to Maggie's grey hair, smeared across her face and spreading over the front of her bright yellow T-shirt. Her hands were covered in blood. Large splotches of red had soaked into the beige carpet. A pink step stool lay on its side behind Maggie. She was surrounded by shoe boxes. Some with lids intact and others spilling their contents. Papers, cards, photos and letters were scattered about.

"Mom. It's okay. I'm here. We'll get help. I'll call the police." Lizzie knelt down but only reached out a shaking hand. Then gathering herself she pulled a red shirt hanging from the bottom rod and wadded it up for a makeshift pillow.

"What's happening?" Maggie said in a raspy whisper, her breathing quick and shallow.

"It's okay Mom. I'm here. Everything's going to be alright," Lizzie said her tone soft but sure. She didn't want to leave her for a second yet she had to get to the phone.

"How did this happen?" Maggie pleaded looking down at the blood on her shirt. "What am I going to do?"

Lizzie could barely hear her mother's words but the fear was evident. "Mom, it's me, Lizzie. I'm going to get the phone from your bed and call the police. They'll send an ambulance. You've fallen and you're bleeding. I need to call 911. The police..."

"Noooo," a low wailing sound came from Maggie as she lay on the floor. "You can't let them take me. Oh dear God. Jesus, Mary and Joseph help me." Terror filled Maggie's eyes and she grabbed at Lizzie's face. "Darling, please no. You help me."

"I'll call an ambulance and we'll take you to the hospital." Lizzie took her mother's bloody hands in her own and spoke gently to her. "I can't help you. Calm down, please."

"No police. Not now," Maggie gasped, her hands trembling and flailing about wildly.

"Mom the police will send the ambulance. I'm just going over to the phone by the bed. I'm right here," Lizzie soothed as she got up and grabbed the phone from the night stand, dialing 911 as she returned to her mother on the floor.

"You help me. Don't call the police," Maggie said trying desperately to get up.

"Mom, stop," Lizzie said then spoke into the phone to the 911 operator. "Her name is Margaret Malone."

"Don't let them come here," said Maggie grasping Lizzie's arm so tightly her nails nearly split the skin.

Trying to ignoring the pain and the anguish in her mother's eyes, Lizzie spoke again to the operator. "She is eighty-five. She fell and hit her head. She's bleeding. Yes, she's conscious."

"What are you telling them? Please help me," Maggie begged, tears now running down her cheeks, mixing with the smudged lipstick around her mouth.

"I need you to stay on the line until the paramedics arrive," the operator told Lizzie.

"I have to get off the phone. I have to help her," Lizzie said panic beginning to overtake her.

"You can help her more by answering my questions. This is information the EMT's need when they arrive." All the while Lizzie answered the questions she patted Maggie's arm and repeated, "It's okay Mom."

Maggie released her hold on Lizzie's arm and turned her head to the side still crying and quivering. Lizzie patted Maggie's arm and tried to reassure her help was on the way.

"The paramedics can access the Knox box for a key to the building but it may be faster if you can buzz them in," the operator told Lizzie. "They have pulled into the parking lot now."

"I can hear the sirens," Lizzie said to the 911 operator. Stroking Maggie's arm and looking directly into her eyes she said "They're here. I'm going to buzz them into the lobby and open your door. I hear the sirens now. Can't you hear them?"

The buzzer sounded loudly and both Lizzie and Maggie jumped. "I'm going to leave for just a minute." Lizzie said as she started to get to her feet. "I have to open the doors. I'll be right back."

"No. Jesus, Mary and Joseph. Don't let them take me," Maggie clutched at Lizzie's hands.

"You'll be fine," Lizzie repeated the words like a mantra as she loosened her mother's fingers from her hand and raced to the front door still holding the phone. She hit the intercom button.

"Come in. We're in 1018. Hurry," she yelled then

turned the deadbolt and opened the door, leaving it ajar.

"I'm coming Mom," Lizzie called out as she pounded down the hall to the master bedroom. Maggie was not on the floor of the closet as Lizzie had left her. She had wiggle to the side, hiding beneath the hanging clothes leaving a trail of papers and blood.

"What are you doing? Please let me help you," Lizzie said as she got down on her knees and tried to untangle Maggie from the mess of bloody shirts and hangers. "I don't know what is happening to you but it will be alright. The EMTs will be here in a minute."

"No. I won't go. You help me. Where is my Sam?" Maggie wailed gripping Lizzie's hand.

Just then the front door opened with a bang and a deep male voice called out, "Ms. Callahan?"

"Back here. It's her head. She fell. She's bleeding." Lizzie could hear the emergency medical technicians talking and pushing the clanking metal stretcher down the large hall. As they entered the bedroom she saw the bags and equipment hanging from the sides.

"Please step aside Ms. Callahan. We'll take it from here," said the young fair skinned woman with the long red hair tied back in a ponytail and a badge that read Bridget.

Maggie trying to burrow further into the closet was crying harder and mumbling. Lizzie understood the words. "Sam, my Sam, where are you?"

"We're here to help. My name is Bridget," the EMT said as she got down on her knees and reached her hand out.

"Bridget? Bridget is that you? Oh thank God. You have to help me," Maggie whimpered.

"That's why I'm here," Bridget said. "Let's get you out of there."

The large master bedroom felt close and cramped with the addition of the six EMTs. Older, broad shouldered and in charge, one of the men separated from the group and took

Lizzie by the arm. "You have blood on your face and hands. Are you hurt?" he asked with concern.

"No," Lizzie said loudly looking down at her hands. "It's mom's blood. Oh God."

"I'm Harry," he said as he steered her to the bathroom. "Why don't you wash that blood off and we can talk. Can you tell me what happened Ms. Callahan?"

Lizzie turned on the tap, pumped a dollop of soap into her hands and looked into the mirror. Her left cheek had three short streaks of blood from where Maggie had grabbed at her. Surprising herself, she started to cry. The fear in her mother's voice, the confusion. It was all so frightening. In the background she could hear the young woman soothing Maggie. Finally, taking a deep breath Lizzie told how she found her mother. She gave him the name of her doctor.

"You say she is confused. Do you think she could have made a mistake with her meds? Can we check her pills?"

Lizzie opened the medicine cabinet on the side wall. It contained they usual items; toothpaste and brush, deodorant, aspirin and bandages in a box. Neatly lined up on the bottom shelf was six bottles of pills and a plastic pill dispenser with a compartment for each day of the week. She pulled down the bottles one by one and handed them to Harry to record the name and dosage.

With the aid of three more EMTs Maggie was now resting on a gurney with a cervical collar around her neck in the middle of the bedroom, talking quietly to the young red headed EMT.

"Oh Jesus, Mary and Joseph. Bridget, I'm so glad you're here," Maggie clutched at Bridget's hand.

"As soon as we finish up here we'll take her to the hospital to be checked out. A head injury should never be ignored. Especially when you say she is sounding so confused," said Harry.

Lizzie leaned back on the granite counter. "My God. Oh Mom"

"Aricept? You didn't mention she had Alzheimer's." Harry put the nearly empty vial of pills on the counter.

"What? Alzheimer's? You must be mistaken," Lizzie nearly shouted as she turned to face Harry. "She doesn't have Alzheimer's."

"That's what this medication is for, Ms. Callahan."

"No. There must be another reason. My mom does not have Alzheimer's." Lizzie said, her voice rising.

"We're almost ready to go here," said Bridget. "We'll be taking Maggie to Largo Medical. I suggest you follow us there."

"I'll ride with you. I can call my husband and brothers from the hospital." Lizzie walked quickly to the side of the gurney and said gently, "Mom, they are..."

"Mom?" Maggie cocked her head and looked directly into Lizzie's eyes. "I'm not your mother," she growled, spittle forming in the corner of her mouth.

There was silence as all faces turned to look at Lizzie.

Stepping back Lizzie put her right hand to her throat. "Mom?"

"Who is that?" Maggie asked Bridget.

"Your daughter, Lizzie," she replied looking down at Maggie.

"I have no daughter. You know that Bridget."

"Is this new behavior?" one of the younger EMTs asked Lizzie with his pen poised over the form on his clipboard.

"Yes." Lizzie ran her hand through her already disheveled hair. "I'm...I'm her only daughter. She has me and my two brothers, Ian and Kevin. My dad died in April."

"I'm sorry," said Harry.

Shaking her head, Lizzie sat down on the beige suede bench at the foot of the king sized bed with the deep purple and vibrant pink spread. She rubbed the soft fabric, seeming to draw comfort from the touch. Looking up, she focused her gaze on Harry. "What happens now?"

"Maggie's agitated. I think it best you meet us there."

"But..." Lizzie spun around to face Bridget, "I can't just let you take her."

"She'll be fine. We're going to Largo Medical," said Harry as he patted Lizzie on the shoulder.

John, another of the EMT's had quietly walked around the condo, checking the other rooms, the cupboards and refrigerator in the kitchen. He looked concerned as he reentered the bedroom. Harry waved him over.

"I took a look around and everything looks neat, clean." Looking down at Lizzie he asked "Are you aware there is very little food in the condo? Just a half loaf of bread and some brown bananas, a few jars of jelly and condiments in the refrigerator. I found several un-opened cans of soup and tuna in the trash along with the can opener. There are opened boxes of crackers and cookies in the cabinet. Not much really."

Lizzie sat staring up at the two men, her hands now mindlessly rubbing her thighs. "I don't know what to say. We have mom over a lot and she still drives. She shops at Publix's, not far from here. How can she not have food?"

Harry nodded and said, "You were unaware of the Alzheimer's until today. Until just now."

Jumping up to face them Lizzie said "We would never leave her without food. We send her home with leftovers. She loves to grocery shop. I know she doesn't cook like she used to but she does cook. Oh my God. I don't know what to say."

"You'll be able to make changes now. This has been quite a shock, but we can see you care for your mother. There are a lot of resources available in the community," Harry said as he turned to survey the situation. "Looks like we're set to go here Ms. Callahan. You can meet us at the hospital. She's going to be okay."

Walking behind the gurney through the condo Lizzie was quiet. When it rolled through the front door she said softly, "I love you Mom."

Maggie's eyes were closed and her lips moved, mouthing, "My Sam. My Sam."

The door shut. Lizzie was alone in the silent condo. She walked back to the master bedroom and stood next to the open closet strewn with bloody clothes, photos and papers.

"Oh Mom."

Chapter 4

"Dan, I need you to meet me at the hospital. Mom fell. The ambulance just left with her," Lizzie yelled into the phone.

"Calm down Lizzie. Did she break anything? Why didn't you go with her?" he said in his reassuring tone.

"I...I don't think she broke anything. She hit her head, a lot of blood. Blood everywhere Dan. They didn't want me to go with her," Lizzie said now almost a whisper as her eyes filled with tears.

"What do you mean they didn't want you to?"

"Dan it's awful. She has Alzheimer's," Lizzie sobbed.

"Lizzie you do not get Alzheimer's from hitting your head. She's probably just shaken up some. Don't cry, honey. You can't drive all upset," Dan said.

"It is Alzheimer's. It's the medication she is on. I'm leaving for Largo Medical. Can you meet me?" Tears were flowing and she wiped them away with the back of her hand. "She didn't know me. She said I wasn't her daughter."

"Lizzie, calm down. Take it easy."

"It is Alzheimer's. She's taking medication you only take if you have Alzheimer's." Lizzie shouted, clutching the phone tightly and pacing the kitchen floor.

"Okay honey. Take it easy. We'll work this out. I'm helping George repair his lawn mower. We have parts everywhere. Let me finish up. Have you called your brothers?"

"Not yet," Lizzie said stopping to lean against the counter. "Dan, what are we going to do?"

"I don't know. We'll figure it out. Call your brothers and have them meet you at the hospital. Will you be okay to drive?" he asked.

"Yes, I'll be okay. I'm just upset," Lizzie said reaching for a tissue. "Confused and scared."

"Call me when you get to the hospital."

"Oh, Dan. Nothing can happen to Mom. It just can't," Lizzie said as she started pacing again. There was a long pause then after a deep breath she said "I'll call Ian and Kevin now."

"It'll be okay Lizzie. I love you," Dan said.

"I love you, too."

Lizzie dialed Ian's cell and got voice mail. She left a short message asking him to call but didn't say why. Then she tried Kevin. He answered on the second ring.

"Hey Lizzie Lou. How are you?"

"Mom's on her way to the hospital. She fell, cut her head. I found her in the closet."

"Fell in the closet. Is she hurt? Are you with her?"

"No, they wouldn't let me go with her. I'm driving over there now. Oh Kevin, it's really bad."

"What did she break? Is she in a lot of pain?"

"She didn't break anything. Hit her head. Kevin she has Alzheimer's," Lizzie blurted.

"What? She fell. How can you say she has Alzheimer's? A lot of older people fall," he stated.

"It's the medication. You only take it if you have Alzheimer's."

"What medication?" Kevin asked.

"Aricept. You only take it if you have Alzheimer's." Lizzie choked.

"Lizzie this doesn't make any sense. It'll take me a few minutes to get to the hospital. I'm just coming back from the office. I'll meet you in the ER. Did you call Ian?"

"Voice mail. I left a message."

"I'll call him too. Take it easy and I'll see you in a few

minutes."

Lizzie drove her Miata just over the speed limit. She had the top down from the earlier drive to the condo. Her long hair was tied back in a clip but still blowing about. On the car ride over Lizzie called Maggie's long time physician, Dr. Anthony Thomas. Of course on a Sunday his office was closed.

"Dr. Anthony Thomas's answering service. How can I help you?" Came the chirpy female voice over the line.

Lizzie tried not to cry as she explained about her mom's fall and confusion and the call for the ambulance.

"So she's at the emergency room?"

"Yes, but I don't know if they'll keep her. I'm on my way now."

"Well, since the emergency is being handled at the ER do you need to talk to him today, on a Sunday? Maybe he could call you during business hours on Monday?"

"Sure. Don't want to disturb the good doctor on his day off," Lizzie responded, her voice tight with anger.

"I don't mean it like that. I just mean it is Sunday. Of course the doctor will call you if you want."

"Never mind. Have him call me on Monday," Lizzie growled as she hit disconnect and threw the phone on to the passenger seat.

Chapter 5

Maggie had already been taken away for a CAT scan when Lizzie was escorted to the curtained cubical by a young nurse with short cropped hair and told to wait.

"Can you tell me anything?" Lizzie she asked holding her purse to her chest like a shield.

"I'm sorry but I don't have any information on your mother. She'll be back here shortly and then the doctor will talk to you," the nurse said with a smile. "Just wait in here."

The ER cubical was big enough to hold a gurney, a night stand and several large trash containers, one deep red with Hazardous Waste written in oversize black letters on each side. Why would they need something so huge Lizzie wondered? God, what's happening here? She tossed her purse on the floor in the corner and leaned against the wall taking a deep breath, letting it out slowly. Once more, breathing in and out, reminding herself to calm down. Thoughts of her mother and father tumbled through her mind and she rocked off the wall and began to pace.

Rickety cart wheels came rolling down the tiled hallway and hushed hospital voices could be heard on the other side of the curtains. She was thinking what wretched places ERs were when she heard Kevin thanking the same pretty nurse for her assistance. Just as she stepped out of the curtained cubical Kevin came near and hugged her tight, patting her back.

"I talked to Ian. Told him what happened. The fall. The diagnosis," he said in a low voice. "You know Ian. He was all bluster and outrage."

Just then the elevators across the hall opened and the

gurney with her mom was pushed out. Kevin moved quickly to the side and took her hand.

"Hello dear. I'm so sorry to be a bother," Maggie said as she smiled up at her youngest son. "Are you my doctor?"

"Mom, it's me Kevin," he said, his eyes wide. With his free hand he pointed to his chest and grimaced, "Your son, Kevin."

Maggie looked around the hall and her lips began to quiver then she said in a small voice, "Of course, dear. It must be the lighting. Of course you are. Why are you here?"

Looking to his sister for support he said, "Lizzie called me. She told me you fell and I came right over. Ian will be here soon. Everything will be okay Mom."

"Ian?" Maggie asked looking around confused then said "Of course it will darling," Her smile was weak but she continued to holding on to his hand.

* * *

Ian strode in shoving the curtains aside. "Mom, how are you?" he asked quickly taking her hand as Lizzie and Kevin stood on the opposite side of the gurney.

"Oh, I'm fine. I don't know what the fuss is about," Maggie groaned. "I need to get back to my condo. I was in the middle of something. I have things to do and don't want to stay here. Can you take me home?"

Ian's smile didn't make it to his fear filled eyes. "We have to wait and see what the doctor says. Do you remember what happened?"

Maggie looked small and delicate as she lay propped up with pillows on the raised bed, covered by starched white sheets. Her right hand fingered the delicate cross at her neck.

"No." She didn't look at him or the others, just over to the blank wall by the curtain. "Bridget was there. She helped me. I don't know where she is now but she helped me."

Ian turned to Lizzie, "Whose Bridget?"

"The EMT. Mom acted as if she knew her and was so relieved she was there. She refused to let me come with her because Bridget was there," said Lizzie sounding like a jealous ten year old.

"How about you and I go get a cup of coffee and leave Ian and Mom here for a few minutes," Kevin said as he took Lizzie's arm and steered her past the curtain. "You look like you could use a break. It had to be awful to find her like that."

The words of support and the strong arm of her younger brother allowed Lizzie the luxury of tears. "Oh Kevy, it was awful," she said calling him by the childish name only she used. "This whole thing is awful."

"Come on. We'll get out of here and talk."

Lizzie leaned against him as they made their way out of the elevator and down the hall to the hospital cafeteria. Kevin settled Lizzie at Formica topped table and went for two cups of strong black coffee. She turned to watch an older gentleman dressed in crisp beige slacks and a soft blue golf shirt holding the arm of an attractive elderly woman, walk slowly to a nearby table. She was wearing white slacks and a brightly printed floral blouse buttoned down the front. Her steel grey hair was short and stylish, her jewelry tasteful. The nails on her hands and the toes that peaked out of cute flat sandals were painted a soft melon color. He pulled out the chair and helped her to sit. They were an elegant couple probably here to visit a friend Lizzie thought. That should be Mom and Dad she almost said aloud. She wasn't trying to eavesdrop as she leaned her elbows on the table and propped her chin in her clasped hands, just think about someone else for a few minutes.

"Joan, we'll get through this. We will. With Paula and the new baby gone, Martin will need our help. Those three little kids will need their grandma and grandpa more now than ever."

My God, thought Lizzie, startled as she realized the horror of what she had just heard. She didn't want to lose her mother but Maggie had lived her life. What if this was her Gabby or Katy or one of the twins? One of her grandchildren? She sat up straighter and looked around the crowded cafeteria. Many of the tables were filled with hospital staff eating their lunch or sitting to rest with a quick coffee. The rest held family and friends of patients. These people looked scared, tired, hopeful and hopeless. They stared at untouched plates of food or numbly moved a cup to their lips. Their conversations were whispered but the feeling of anguish was evident on their faces. Lives were being altered by what was happening elsewhere in this enormous building.

"Alzheimer's? Lizzie, are you sure?" Kevin asked as he set the steaming mug of coffee in front of her.

She looked up, momentarily surprised to see him. "Yes. Alzheimer's. Kevin, that's what the EMT said. No one takes Aricept unless they have Alzheimer's." Shaking her head she reached out to pick up the coffee. Tears welled in her eyes and threatened to fall but she took a deep breath and tried to brace herself against the onslaught of emotion roiling within.

"Dad had to know. Who else knew? Did Phyllis?" Kevin asked pulling out the chair to sit. "Why wouldn't Dad tell us? Did he think we couldn't handle it?"

"No one told me. Phyllis didn't say a word. I've talked to her a bit since Dad died but she never said anything. I can't imagine she wouldn't tell us." Lizzie held the hot mug in her hands and sipped the steaming black liquid. "I needed coffee, maybe something stronger even," she suggested.

Kevin set his cup on the table. "I'm still stuck on Dad not telling us. If she was taking medication, Dad had to know," he said the worry lines creasing his forehead. "We need to talk to her doctor. Has he called back?"

"Not yet. He will," she said, the tears now filling her eyes ran down her cheeks. "Oh Kevin, I don't know what to do. It was all so strange. It was like she didn't know me. She didn't trust me. She was screaming not to call the police."

Kevin said reaching over to touch his sister's arm. "Don't cry Lizzie. We'll sort it out. The hit on the head confused her. You know Mom has always been a bit leery around police. Remember when Ian said he wanted to be a cop and she told him over her dead body. I figured she didn't want to worry about a son risking his life every day. Who knows maybe she has something to hide," he joked.

* * *

Lizzie steeled herself to make the call to Phyllis. They had to get some answers, if there were any.

"Hi Phyllis. It's Lizzie. I don't know if you heard about Mom. She had a fall and is at Largo Medical in the ER. She's going to be okay but... I need to ask you about her."

There was silence on the line and Lizzie asked, "Are you there?"

Phyllis blurted out "I'm sorry Lizzie. I know about the Alzheimer's. I should have said something."

"You knew? And said nothing?" hissed Lizzie as she stood in the corridor outside her mother's curtained cubical.

"Lizzie, your dad told me two weeks before he died. One evening she seemed off to me. You know how certain your mom is about everything? That night she seemed a bit dazed. I was worried so I asked him if everything was alright. At first he didn't say anything; just that Maggie was probably tired. Then he broke down and cried. He promised me to secrecy. I'm sorry for not telling you but I didn't know how. I ...I guess I thought her doctor would talk to you. Lizzie, I know I'm a silly old woman. I'm sorry. I..."

Lizzie could hear the fear and sadness in the voice of her mom's best friend. "Oh Phyllis," she sighed and walking further down the hall. This is all too much she thought running her hand through her hair.

"Maggie's like my own sister. I'd do anything for her," said Phyllis the distress evident in her quivering voice.

"I know," Lizzie said. She waited silently as Phyllis cried and apologized again. "It'll be okay. I have to get back to mom now. The nurse has finished up with her for the time being. I'll call you later. She'll be at my house for a few days, you can come visit. Don't worry. We'll work it out."

Disconnecting the phone she leaned against the wall hoping she would not fall. Her world was coming apart and she didn't know how to gather the pieces together again. For the hundredth time since finding her mother in the closet she wished her dad was there. Straightening her spine and taking a deep breath she pulled herself from the wall and walked towards the curtain to face her mom and brothers.

* * *

About an hour later, Maggie's children huddled in the hall and quietly decided her fate.

"She is coming home with me for a week or so. Until she heals," Lizzie insisted. "I'll take her to see Dr. Thomas next week and get some answers."

"She keeps saying she wants to go home," Kevin said. "What'll you tell her?"

"Mom doesn't get a choice here, Kevin. She can't go home alone. Not now." Ian was adamant, his hands in his pockets jiggling the keys and coins. "We need to start making arrangements. Day care, home care, a facility even."

Lizzie held up her hands "Stop. Right now. We don't know what's going on. We need answers before we start changing her world and our worlds. Let's get Mom to my house for a few days and go from there."

"Lizzie, you can't care for her by yourself. You work.

We all do. We need to make plans for the safety and sanity of everyone," Ian cautioned.

"I know that Ian," Lizzie snapped, "but we have no idea what we are dealing with. We didn't know about the Alzheimer's until a few hours ago and now you're talking about a facility?"

Sounding defensive he said, "I don't mean now. Just we need to plan for down the road. Dad isn't here and well, I guess we don't know what he was going to do and now we need to decide...."

"Exactly. We have no idea at all about anything," Kevin barked. "Lizzie's right. Let her take her home, meet with the doctor and get some answers. We don't have to make any decisions right now." Reaching over to pat his older brother's arm Kevin said in a quieter voice, "Let's all take a breath here and relax..."

"What's happening?" Maggie called out, her voice bristling with anger. "What plans are you making? You don't run my life, you know. I want to go home."

Ian drew back the curtain and stepped close to the gurney. "The doc wants someone with you. You had a nasty hit on the head, Mom. He won't release you unless you come to stay with one of us. Lizzie wants you to go home with her for a few days."

"She doesn't have time for me," Maggie barked, pointing a shaking finger at Lizzie. "I'll be fine at the condo. I slipped and fell. It could've happened to any of you. I want to go home." Maggie struggled to sit up and swing her legs over the side of the bed.

"Not so fast. You have to stay until the doctor releases you. We only want what's best."

"You don't know anything," Maggie yelled.

"Mom, you need a little extra care now. Come home with Kevin or me. It doesn't have to be Lizzie. You can't stay alone," Ian stated in his most authoritative voice while gently reaching for Maggie's shoulders.

She slapped his hands away and demanded, "What are you talking about?"

"You need someone with you," Kevin interjected, trying to pull her back onto the pillows.

"I don't need anyone, especially all of you telling me what to do," Maggie declared settling back in the bed. "Of course I can be alone. I'm fine."

"I'm taking the week off work. Things have been slower and we could spend the time together," Lizzie said from the foot of the bed. "We'll have fun. Besides I could use a break and you know what great fun we always have. We'll go to lunch and maybe some shopping," she said trying to smile.

Maggie snorted and crossed her arms as best she could with the IV needle still in her arm. "Fine. But only for a few days. I have things to do at home."

Just then the curtain was swept aside and the ER doctor arrived to tell the family he didn't think Maggie would be admitted to the hospital. The scans and x-rays results came back normal.

"Broken bones at her age are a serious concern but she landed on soft plush carpet. The cut on the back of her head, though bloody was not serious. A few stitches were required. The other scrapes and bruises will heal without any further treatment," he stated. "You can go home with one of your children, Mrs. Malone. Take it easy on them, please. They just want to help."

"Of course, Doctor. Whatever you think it best. I'll be going home with her," Maggie purred nodding towards Lizzie. "Thank you for everything Doctor."

The three children exchanged grateful glances as the doctor left the room. Maggie was of the generation who respected and obeyed doctors. She waited quietly in the bed till the nurse came to help her dress for home.

Chapter 6

Lizzie's oldest daughter, Gabby, glared as she stood with one hand on her hip and the other tightly holding a cup of coffee. "Mom you don't need to do this alone. Why did you have kids? You had kids to help out. That's what Daddy always said. Of course we were not always helpful, but now, let me be here for you."

"How did you even know I was going to Grand Maggie's today?" Lizzie asked taking a sip of her coffee.

"Daddy told me Uncle Kevin was taking Grand Maggie this morning to give you a break. And, instead of you taking it easy you were going to the condo to clean it up. The kids went to a sleep over and are going to Busch Gardens. You should not do this alone."

"Alright Gabby you can help. We'll take two cars in case you have to leave."

Nodding her head, Gabby put down her coffee and leaned over to give Lizzie a hug.

* * *

Both women found guest parking spots by the street. Lizzie grabbed the plastic tote filled with cleaning supplies from the trunk. Gabby was right behind her pulling out a bag of rags and paper towels. They walked towards the building but stopped to look at the large in-ground pool and the shimmering Gulf of Mexico beyond.

"I remember coming here to swim when I was little.

Grandpa Sam would play with us on the beach. He would go running into the waves then come roaring back to the sand like a sea monster," Gaby said smiling and shading her eyes from the glare.

Lizzie continued to gaze at the water remembering the sight of her larger than life father, dripping with water and sea weeds emerge from the waves and chase the grandchildren up the sandy beach. Wiping away a lone tear she turned to Gabby. "He loved you Gee Kids. I never remember him so free with your uncles and me but by the time you kids came along he was a changed man. Easier and more relaxed. Grand Maggie too."

"Come on Mom. If we stand here much longer we'll end up down there on the beach reminiscing. We have work to do," said Gabby as she hugged Lizzie with her free arm.

They rode the elevator in silence. No neighbors were around as they walked to the door with the Life is a Beach sign hanging from a seashell hook. Lizzie fumbled with the key.

"Here, let me," Gabby said as she took the jangling keys from Lizzie's shaking hand and opened the door. She moved into the kitchen and dropped her bags on the granite counter.

Lizzie halted after taking only three steps. She looked around, wanting someone to be there, wanting to hear a voice call from the balcony or back bedroom. Rarely had she been in the condo without her mom or dad. Feeling like a trespasser she moved into the kitchen. The sound of the air conditioner turning on caused her to jump then smile in embarrassment.

Watching from across the room Gabby asked "Are you okay?"

"Sure, I'm fine," replied Lizzie feigning lightheartedness with a smile and laugh she didn't feel.

"I'll make a pot of coffee while we figure out what to do here," said Gabby.

Without waiting for a reply Gabby rinsed out the pot and filled the Mr. Coffee with water. "I brought some Godiva chocolate coffee. I know you like it."

"Oh Gabby, you are so sweet," Lizzie said sitting at the table, elbows on the lemon colored quilted place mats, resting her chin in her hands. "I know this is a delaying tactic. We should be in the closet right now cleaning but this is nice, normal."

"It's alright to be normal for a few minutes. We'll drink our coffee in the bedroom," said Gabby as she picked up the cleaning supplies and strode down the hall towards the master bedroom.

"Come on Mom," Gaby said stepping in the room. Walking directly to the closet she flipped the light on. "Wow."

Lizzie following behind, faltered at the door.

"Oh my God. It's worse than I remember," Lizzie said dropping the supplies on the floor as she surveyed area. Look at this mess."

Clothes were strewn about the floor of the closet and the bedroom, some dangling precariously from hangers. The pink ladder had been moved to a corner of the bedroom, probably by the EMTs. At least thirty cardboard shoe boxes were piled haphazardly on the blood stained beige carpet. Some contained smart looking flat sandals or white canvas espadrilles. Other boxes, faded and worn, were filled with papers and photos that had spilled all over the floor.

"What is all this?" asked Gabby pointing to the photos and papers.

"I have no idea. Grand Maggie must have used the boxes to store her memories. Let's get them back in the boxes and we go through them later. We have to get the bloody clothes out of here. I hope we can get the stains out of them and the carpet. I didn't remember this much blood," Lizzie said standing by the closet door and holding on the jamb for support.

"We'll get it done," said Gabby bringing over the laundry basket and picking clothes off the floor. Looking up at the back of the closet she saw half a dozen golf shirts. "Grandpa Sam," she pointed with a sad smile.

Lizzie turned to look. "Oh, I never realized Grand Maggie kept those. Your uncles helped her bag up Daddy's clothes for donation to Your Neighborhood Thrift Store on 9th Avenue. I thought we got rid of everything. I can understand her keeping a few of his shirts. The scents. The memories. They liked to golf together even though she was not very good and he was terrific," said Lizzie laughing. "They loved being together, adored each other. You see that in the beginning of relationships but for them it was always there. As if they shared a special secret. Even when they were angry at each other Daddy would go to her, take her hand or bend down to kiss her cheek. 'There, there honey, there, there,' he would say and just like that, like magic," Lizzie said snapping her fingers, "Mom would smile. Maybe not a big one but it was there tugging at the corners of her mouth and glinting in her eyes. She would still be mad, an easier, gentler mad and the anger would be gone. They picked their battles and it seemed to me they were few and far between."

"Grandpa Sam was a gentleman, so handsome and clever," said Gabby. "He was good to us Gee Kids. Our friends all loved him. I think half my girlfriends wished he was their grandpa. He didn't patronize us or make long winded when-I-was- your-age speeches. He told us funny stories to make his point and listened to ours even when we were obnoxious teenagers, so full of ourselves."

Once the clothes were off the floor, the cardboard shoe boxes and scattering of photos and papers remained. "What a mess this is," sighed Lizzie.

"Why don't you see what you can do with the laundry? I'll put this stuff back in the boxes then up on the shelves. You don't want to go through any of this now do you?" Gabby asked.

"No, I can't, "Lizzie said shaking her head. "I just can't

face it now and I don't feel comfortable going through her things. We'll save it for another day. Maybe when she's feeling better we can sit down and go through the old photos and reminisce." Picking up the basket she said, "I want to get the clothes clean. I don't know if we will ever get this blood out. I'll use some of the stuff you brought to pretreat these stains."

On hands and knees, Gabby started picking up the scattered papers and photos and placed them back in the boxes. There were yellowed envelopes with elegant handwriting and foreign postage stamps, old black and white photos of people and places she did not recognize. Some were marred with dried blood. Others creased and faded. She came to a photo of a tall handsome young man in an army uniform with a dark haired beauty in a light colored dress standing in front of a store front with a wooden door and a large plate glass window lettered with the words 'The Pub'. Grandpa Sam and Grand Maggie. So young, younger than George and I thought Gabby. She set it aside and continued working till all the boxes were full and tucked neatly back on the shelves.

"Do you think Grand Maggie would mind if I took this?" asked Gabby showing the photo of the young couple to Lizzie. "I'll get a copy made and give it back. It's just that I don't ever remember seeing a photo of them in London. Grandpa sure was handsome. Look at Grand Maggie, so beautiful. Theirs is such a romantic story, Mom. A young couple meets during the war, fall in love, get married, move to America and live happily ever after."

"It is a wonderful love story Gabby, but I'm not so sure about happily ever after," sighed Lizzie. "Oh, they had their problems like every married couple. You don't raise three kids without some tension and arguments. But look what's going on now. Grandpa is gone and now Grand Maggie falling..."

"It's going to be okay," interrupted Gabby as she tucked the photo in her purse. Walking over to her mom she embraced her in a tight hug and kissed her cheek. "Let me take some of this laundry home with me. Between the two of us we'll get it done faster."

Chapter 7

Lizzie owned a small real estate office on the beach with a partner, Samantha Sweet. With a voice that matched her name Samantha drawled into the phone, "Honey, you take all the time you need. Things are fabulous here. We have buyers coming in from out of town but I've got help. Ray and Mindy are both willing to take on new clients. Our new girl, Amy, is working out fine. She is a dream come true with the paperwork. Maggie's the priority. You take care of her and yourself. We'll talk later in the week."

Putting the phone down Lizzie smiled. The household had quickly settled into a routine. Maggie was up early but stayed in her room until Dan left for work. Then she and Lizzie ate their bagels and fruit sitting together at the breakfast bar. Conversation was light, talk of the Gee Kids or some household chore that needed to be done. Maggie took short naps in the early afternoon then went to the family room to sit by the window looking out at the Gulf with an unopened book in her lap. Pepper, the sleek black cat Lizzie and Dan adopted from the shelter several years before, lay curled at her feet. The cat followed Maggie through the house. She would slip into the bedroom when the door was ajar, leap on the bed and meow softly to get Maggie's attention. In the evenings, as they sat in the family room watching TV or talking, Pepper would jump on Maggie's lap. Gently petting the cat on the top of her head Maggie would repeat, "Pretty kitty." Lizzie had smiled to herself watching this cozy scene because before the fall in the closet, Maggie had never liked cats, especially Pepper. And, Pepper hadn't like Maggie either.

Over the past few days Lizzie had repeated her carefully worded explanation about Maggie not being alone. Each time it was met with stony silence. Now, late in the afternoon, Lizzie busied herself in the kitchen making a pot of English Breakfast Tea and setting peanut butter and oatmeal cookies on a plate.

From the family room Maggie hollered, "Ian had no right to talk to you and Kevin about me. I can take care of myself. I do not want to hear about your plans. I raised my family and helped raise yours. I don't want to be a burden. I want the last few years of my life to be peaceful not drama filled. I won't have all of you hanging around my condo, poking into things, telling me what to do. All those young kids would bring their loud music and silly movies and stuff into my home. They're noisy and never sit still," Maggie complained, her hands balled into fists in her lap. "I like my time alone, my peace and quiet."

"Those young kids are your grandchildren and great grandchildren," Lizzie gently reminded Maggie.

"Don't you think I know? Don't you think I can remember anything? I may be a bit loony but I still know who my family is," Maggie stated. "They are just too much for me to handle. I know the parents want to get out and leave the babies with me but I just can't do it any more Lizzie. I just can't."

"It's not like that Mom," Lizzie smiled bringing the tray laden with goodies to the family room. "Let's have some tea and cookies." Cookies. Unbelievable. Just like I do when trying to quiet my grandchildren Lizzie thought.

All of our elaborate planning is going nowhere Lizzie mused as she and Maggie sipped their tea and ate the peanut butter and oatmeal cookies from her daughter, Gabby. She had baked them especially for Grand Maggie. Those were the first cookies Lizzie remembered making with her mom. And, the first cookie she remembers her mom making with Gabby.

She had been about six at the time and so eager to help Grand Maggie. There were lots of giggles and smiles when Gabby entered the family room carrying a paper plate piled with misshapen, golden brown cookies. She had carefully walked around the room to allow everyone to choose a cookie. There was much oohing and smacking of lips over the delicious treats as Gabby stood by grinning. Grandpa Sam said they were so good she could go into business and make a fortune. Instead of Famous Amos it would be Fabulous Gabby. Smiling to herself, Lizzie was grateful for the wonderful memories.

"I want you to stay another week. Dan is golfing in a tournament next Saturday and will be out late. The two of us can have the day together. Just you and me. We can go shopping down to John's Pass and have lunch while we watch the pelicans and dolphins. Or garage sales? We have not hit the garage sales for a while. And, I think St. Joes is having a rummage sale. It will be fun. Like old times," Lizzie said.

Maggie eyed her with suspicion and didn't speak for several minutes as she sipped tea and munched on a cookie. Placing the tea cup on the table she looked at Lizzie with a tight smile and nodded her head. "Alright, I'll stay a few more days."

"Excellent. We'll have a great week," Lizzie replied smiling.

"Will I be able to go to Mass on Sunday?" asked Maggie.

"Of course," said Lizzie.

Picking up her tea and peering into the cup Maggie asked in a soft voice, "Will I be able to go to confession on Saturday?"

Looking amused Lizzie said, "Mom, you're in your 80's. What could you possibly have to confess?"

Maggie's dark green eyes clouded over as she lifted her face to look directly at Lizzie. In a voice quivering with fear she said "You don't know what I have done."

Chapter 8

The weekend started out well. Dan was home when Lizzie and Maggie arrived Friday evening. They had gone back to the condo to gather more clothes for the extra days. Maggie didn't seem to notice anything amiss in the closet as they had picked out pants and tops to pack. Lizzie wasn't sure if she noticed the brown stains on the carpet or chose to ignore them. After hugs and kisses all around, Dan headed out the door to get the bags from the car and take them to the guest room. Maggie had helped decorate that room. After the last of the kids left home, Lizzie decided she wanted a room of her own. An elegant guest room but one she could use.

"Every room is yours. All I get is the garage and the deck," Dan teased, though he didn't really care. Lizzie had made their home a showplace. Not with wildly expensive pieces but with creativity and charm.

Lizzie had the plan laid out for the room so there was no scene in the fabric store about clowns or gators. The room was soothing in pale greens, beige and multiple shades of purple from deepest eggplant to the faintest violet. There was a queen size walnut sleigh bed with too many pillows, large side tables and wall mounted lamps that were perfect for reading. A moss green overstuffed chair and matching foot stool was next to a floor lamp. Books of all kinds from mysteries and biographies to crafts and growing herbs filled the shelves which covered the walls. A small roll top desk with cubbies and drawers sat by the window. Lizzie loved to sit there writing letters and look out over the backyard with its many shades of green interspersed with the bright tropical hibiscus, birds of paradise and view of the ever changing blue Gulf waters. She knew her mom found this room and the expansive sight restful. She hoped the peacefulness would help keep Maggie calm.

Lizzie put her mom's clothes in the drawers and closet and her toiletries in the private bath. This was to be a temporary situation but she knew plans change and flexibility was going to be the word of the day for weeks and months and maybe years to come. The sudden death of her father just a few months ago still had her reeling. Now with her mom's unbelievable diagnosis she was acutely aware of life's complications and fragility.

How could they not have known of Maggie's condition? Looking back it seems so obvious. She would forget the name of someone she had known for years. When you're my age you'll forget a thing or two she would say with a lighthearted smile. When she had trouble reading the paper she blamed it on the cataract surgery from two years before. Should never have let anyone mess with my eyes she would say then change the subject.

Sam had known and helped Maggie with the deception. "Look Maggie, here comes Lizzie and Dan. Here's another grandchild. So many Gee-kids Grand Maggie, it's hard to remember them all by name. Which one are you darling?" he would say with that mischievous smile and wink. It worked great. None of them suspected a thing.

Lizzie kept the day's low key. Quick visits from Ian or Kevin. Rose and Becca stopped by more to support Lizzie than visit with their mother-in-law. They could accept the diagnosis better than their spouses. One by one the Gee-kids called, wanting to see Grand Maggie but understood when Lizzie said no, she needs to rest. They had not been told the diagnoses. The three adult children did not fully believe it themselves so they could not talk to the rest of the family. Amongst themselves they decided to perpetuate the deception started by their father.

* * *

On Saturday morning Maggie was on the move soon after Dan left. She was out of the shower, dressed and ready for an adventure by 9:00. This was her first outing except for the one follow-up with Dr. Thomas and Mass on Sunday. The bruising on her face was minimal, covered up with foundation and her hair hid the stitches at the back of her head.

The two women sat at the breakfast bar in the whitewashed bentwood stools. Everyone vied for one of those stools at family gatherings, especially the Gee-kids. The arms and backs meant you were safe as you twirled around and around. The kitchen was large but still felt cozy even with the spectacular view of the Gulf. No walls, just windows and sliding glass doors leading to the deck and pool. At the water's edge was a large multilevel dock. Dan had drawn up the plans for the remodel after he and Lizzie bought the house ten years earlier. They lived through two years of construction, upheaval and mess to have their perfect home.

Sam would show up at odd hours during the day to chat with the workmen. Maggie would be with him bringing home-made cookies. She got to know the men, knew about their wives and kids. She even made extra cookies for the men to take home. "Lizzie," she would say, "If you make them feel special they will treat you special and take extra care with the jobs they are doing."

The women shared a light breakfast of fruit and wheat toast with apple butter. Hot tea for Maggie and strong black coffee for Lizzie.

"Why are you drinking black coffee?" Maggie demanded. "No self-respecting Irishman would start the day without a good cup of tea with cream and sugar."

"I've been drinking coffee for years Mom," Lizzie

replied. "I used to have a cup with Daddy when I was a teenager. He sure loved his coffee but he drank it way too sweet, three spoons of sugar. I remember the big blue sugar bowl on the counter."

At the mention of Sam, Maggie's shoulders dropped and the spark in her eyes seemed to dull. Looking down at her hands she whispered, "My Sam."

* * *

The weather was good but a bit too warm to garage sale so they headed over to the rummage sale at St. Joes. Maggie and Sam played bingo there often so she was known by a few of the men and women running the event. From years attending the sales they knew Lizzie too. Sofas and beds as well as tires and lawn mowers were located in the parking lot where men from the church roamed around offering advice and help loading up the goods in car trunks. Several waved to Lizzie and Maggie as the two women walked towards the left side of the church heading back to the school auditorium. Maggie halted. Looking around she asked, "Where are we?"

"St. Joes."

"St. Joes? Are we here for confession?" Maggie asked touching the cross at her neck.

"No. The Rummage Sale is today," Lizzie said taking her mom by the arm.

"Can I go to confession?" Maggie asked holding tight to the cross at her neck.

"Not now. We're here for the sale."

"What sale? You told me I could go to confession," insisted Maggie.

"Not now. I'll take you later today, I promise," Lizzie said, gently pulling Maggie along.

Today was bag day at the sale. Everything you could put in a big brown paper grocery bag was $5.00. Lizzie and Maggie loved the hunt for treasures. Vintage clothes, sewing patterns, boxes of buttons, record albums, odd dishes, books and just plain old junk. Lizzie felt a link to the past owners. Someone had bought and used and possibly treasured these items. Whenever anyone commented on a lovely dish or table cloth she was using it was probably one picked up at a rummage sale or a thrift store. Lizzie explained it away by saying "It's been in the family for years," but not bothering to say whose family.

"How did you meet Dan?" asked Maggie as she and Lizzie surveyed a table laden with serving platters.

"At school Mom. You remember." As the words left her lips she wished she could bring them back. No, if she remembered she would not be asking, you idiot, Lizzie thought to herself.

Maggie seemed not to notice as she asked, "Didn't he live outside of Kells? On ... on...what was the street? The farm... not all the way to Navin?"

"I don't know where that is," Lizzie answered leaning over to pick up a clear cut glass plate.

"Of course you do, Navin is just south of Kells. We've walked there together many times. Remember we once wanted to walk to Dublin," Maggie said with a mischievous grin.

"Dublin?" Lizzie asked. Turning to look at her mom she said "Dan's never been to Ireland. Neither have I."

"Really?" Maggie cocked her head and eyed Lizzie. "Well if you say so.."

Lizzie looked closely at the plate in her hand and then over to her mom. "No, he's never been to Ireland."

"Alright dear. But he looks just like a young man I knew there ... before I left for England."

"Who was he?" Lizzie asked.

"Danny. Danny. What was his last name? I thought it was Callahan."

"That's Dan's last name but he has never been to Ireland."

"I knew him for a long time, friend of the family. Lovely young man. I know he helped me, helped my family... I just can't remember with what."

"I don't think it was Dan." Lizzie tried again to explain. "He was born in 1952."

Ignoring Lizzie, Maggie continued, "He was married before, right? Did he have children? I know he wanted them."

"No Mom. Dan was not married before me. He only has our four girls, Gabby, Katy and the twins Shannon and Charlotte. You're confusing him with someone else." Lizzie said taking a deep breath and returning the plate to the table.

"Oh, honey. Maybe he didn't tell you. Maybe he doesn't have other children but I know he was to be married. What could have happened?" Maggie asked, her mouth in a frown and wrinkles forming on her brow.

Lizzie and Maggie continued walking through the school auditorium past dozens of tables piled high with all sorts of goodies. Glassware and dishes were located in one area to the right, while books and games were on the left. Clothes hung on racks at the outer edges. Large handmade signs hung on the wall overhead to indicate men's, women's and children's clothes. Both women holding on to their brown bags proceeded to walk down the center aisle. Lizzie was distracted by the conversation with her mom. She wasn't focusing on the items on the tables but thinking about a young man named Danny who helped her and her family. Helped with what? When? None of this made sense to her.

"Lizzie. Lizzie," a laughing voice called out.

"Georgia!" The two women hugged and yelped and danced a bit. "Oh my God Georgia, when did you get to town? I didn't expect you until late this year."

"We're here for a long weekend. Flew in to see Dean's family. His mom's not doing real well. We're hoping she'll do better once we move here. You know, having Dean around will be a big boost for her. I was going to call but it was such a short visit I didn't know if we would be able to get together. How are you? Where's Maggie? Is she here? I want to give her a hug."

"Maggie's right over there. Georgia, she may not know you. We found out she has Alzheimer's. Good days and bad. Good hours and not so good hours."

"Lizzie, I'm so sorry," said Georgia reaching out to hug Lizzie again. "How awful. I don't know what to say. I... I...Is she living with you? How is everyone coping? How are you doing?"

"Oh Georgia. I wish we had a few hours to talk. It would take that to get it all out. So much has happened so fast. Maggie's alright. We told her but she doesn't remember. Dad knew. He never told us. They thought they could handle it like they did everything else in their lives. Just the two of them. Might have worked if Dad hadn't died. God, listen to me. I sound awful," Lizzie said shaking her head.

"No you don't. This is a load to deal with all at once. Listen, even if we don't get together we can talk on the phone. I'll be in town till Wednesday. You have my cell number. We can ..."

The sound of breaking glass and a woman's scream interrupted their conversation. Lizzie spun around to see her mom, right arm outstretched leaning over the table filled with tall glass bud vases. Several had shattered on the floor and more were rolling towards the table's edge. Both women hurried to Maggie's side.

"That's mine. My Sam gave me that vase. That's mine," shouted Maggie.

"What are you doing? What's the matter with you? It's just a glass vase. They all look alike. I'm sure yours is at home," Lizzie said trying to take Maggie by the arm.

"It's mine. I want it. How did it get here?" demanded Maggie raising her voice and swatting at Lizzie's hand.

"Maggie. It's me, Georgia. Here, let me help you. Is this the one you want?"

Maggie's anger was gone as quickly as it had arrived. With a smile she turned to Georgia. "Yes, that's mine. My Sam gave it to me. He always brought me flowers you know. Flowers for no reason at all. My Sam."

Lizzie was trying to pick up the broken vases but two women from the church arrived with brooms and a dust pan.

"We've got it. Don't worry. Just a few broken vases. No harm done."

"I'll pay for them," Lizzie said as she watched Georgia and her mom, off to the side now, looking at the cheap glass vase. "I'm so sorry. My mom is not herself and my dad..."

The older woman with ash blond hair cut in a stylish bob and intense blue eyes spoke quietly, "Lizzie, I knew your parents. I'm Maureen Donahue. I know what happened. You mom is grieving. Sam was the light of her life and now that he's gone she's trying to hold on to anything. Don't worry Lizzie."

"You knew them?" Lizzie asked in amazement.

"Sure lots of us knew them. Your folks played bingo here and they were involved in the church. They belonged to St. Mary's but they came here for Mass sometimes and social functions. We were all so sorry to hear about Sam."

"My mom has Alzheimer's," Lizzie blurted out. "Oh my God. I didn't mean to say that. We haven't told people. I just wanted you to know she's not crazy with grief ...well not just crazy either. Oh my God. I'm sorry." She didn't know she was crying until Rose reached into the pocket of her flowered print apron and retrieved a packet of tissue. "Here, take one. I'm sorry about your Mom, honey. We didn't know she was ill."

"Please don't say anything. I shouldn't have told you," Lizzie begged as she wiped away the tears.

"Of course not, honey," replied Maureen. "It's our secret."

From across the room Maggie and Georgia were waving

at Lizzie. "I have to go." Lizzie opened her purse and grabbed her wallet. "Here, let me pay you for the vases."

"No. No. Just go take care of Maggie. Take care of yourself, too."

Shaking a bit from the emotional overload Lizzie joined her mother and friend.

"Let's have a cup of tea girls," said Maggie grinning and patting Georgia's arm. "I'm sure they are selling something sweet to eat."

The three women walked to the next room and found a place to sit at one of the long cafeteria tables. The beige metal folding chair scraped on the floor as Georgia pulled it out for Maggie. "Now you sit here Maggie, with me, while Lizzie gets us something. It's so wonderful to see you. How have you been?"

Lizzie hovered over the table laden with home baked goods. Think normal she told herself. The brownies looked tasty and she knew how much Dan loved them. She picked up a flimsy paper plate covered in plastic wrap of six nut-filled, chocolate iced brownies. Zucchini bread. She couldn't remember the last time she had that. One small loaf, maybe two. She could freeze one for later. The chocolate chip cookies look good and the oatmeal too. And a loaf of garlic bread and an apple pie for tonight. Then she selected a plate filled with peanut butter cookies.

This is normal she thought as she picked up the tray filled with the snacks for now and the bag of breads and sweets for later.

Maggie looked expectantly at Lizzie as she approached the table. "I've been telling our friend here about Danny. She said she's not aware of his being married before. I was sure she would remember him, sure she would know what happened to his other wife, if he did get married."

"Mom, Dan's never been married before me," stated Lizzie setting the tray on the table.

"They wanted children, you know."

"Who? Who wanted children? I don't know who you are talking about," Lizzie grumbled.

"Hush. No need to be so loud. We're just talking. My friend here and I were just talking and you barged in."

"Barged in? I went to get cookies and tea. And your friend is my friend Georgia," Lizzie whined pulling out the chair.

"Wow, I've never been fought over before," Georgia cut in with a laugh. "Ladies let's drink the tea before it gets cold and those cookies look delicious."

"Sorry. Go ahead with your story," said Lizzie as she unloaded the cups of hot water, tea bags, tiny cartons of cream and packets of low-cal sweetener.

"Never mind, now," Maggie said as she lowered her head and twisted her hands in her lap.

"Maggie, please tell me about your friend Danny. Did you know him growing up in Ireland?"

"It doesn't matter now," Maggie said still not looking up but reaching for the cross at her neck.

"Ah, but it does Maggie, I would love to hear about him," Georgia pleaded.

Raising her eyes to look directly at Georgia she spoke in a soft voice. "He helped me. I can't remember now what it was all about. It's confusing. But I know he was seeing someone. I don't know what happened. He lived down the lane, down by ... I can't remember. Can you?" she turned to Lizzie.

"No, I can't remember either," said Lizzie feeling guilty for her earlier outburst.

"Well no matter. He's here now. Maybe Danny will tell me what happened..... but I don't want to be nosy."

"Nosy? You Mom?" Lizzie joked.

"Maggie? Nosy?" Georgia said at the same time.

There was an instant of silence then all three of them laughed. Laughed so loud the folks in the nearby tables turned to look. This caused the women to laugh even harder.

Finally, still half laughing, Maggie said, "Stop it girls and drink your tea before it gets cold."

Chapter 9

They arrived home just after noon. Lizzie fixed tuna salad sandwiches and again the two women sat at the breakfast bar to eat. Lizzie wanted to ask more about Danny but knew her mom wouldn't have any answers. Over hot tea, black coffee and a plate of cookies they discussed the morning of bargain hunting. Maggie didn't bring up the trying incident and Lizzie couldn't. This was a peaceful few minutes and she wanted to enjoy them.

"I'm tired, dear. Maybe a short nap is what I need," Maggie said as she picked up the plates and took them to the sink. "A short nap," she repeated.

"Leave that. I'll put them in the dishwasher," said Lizzie.

"That's fine dear," said Maggie moving towards the hall and her room.

Lizzie had things to do and grabbed a pad and pencil from the counter top to write them all down before they slipped from her mind. She drank the last of her coffee, now cold in the mug, but could not make herself get up for another one. She sat staring at the paper, unable to write. Twisting the pencil in her hand she replayed the scene at the church sale. One minute Maggie was fine then she seemed like a different person. Her once kind and easy demeanor slipped away and an angry woman took over. Thank God Georgia came along Lizzie thought. She seemed to have a calming influence over Maggie. Tired of trying to control what no one could control Lizzie picked up the pencil and began to make her list.

* * *

Maggie woke at 2:30 and came quietly into the kitchen. A cup of tea was needed to get her head straight. So many thoughts whirling about. Am I going crazy she wondered. "Hello, hello, is anyone here?" Maggie called with a slight rise in her voice.

"Here Mom, right here. I had just stepped out to get the mail. How about a cup of tea and then I'll take you to confession." Lizzie said coming through the front door.

At 3:30 they headed out to church. It was a short drive to St Mary's. Maggie was quiet but Lizzie was not. She never was. According to her dad she had gotten the gift of gab from Maggie. Dan called her the background noise of his life. She kept up running commentary on all the kids and grandkids. "Emma will start kindergarten this falls. She is very excited to be one of the big kids. Nate promises to take good care of her. He is such a good big brother."

"The kids all love school. So much to do, to learn, seeing their friends. I wanted to be a teacher. What a joy that would have been. Or, a writer. I had stories to tell," Maggie said with a touch of regret in her voice as Lizzie pulled in to the parking lot of the church. Not many cars, so it shouldn't take long for her to go to confession thought Lizzie.

They climbed the grey stone steps and opened the heavy wooden doors. The vestibule was cool and quiet, a pleasant respite from the summer heat. Their heels clicked on the tile floor and echoed in the large church as they walked down the side aisle towards the altar. The confessionals, a wood structure built into the wall with three intricately carved wooden doors with bronze mesh for windows were located on either side of the church towards the front. Father Sullivan was on duty according to the small sign in front of the right confessional. The two women genuflected then moved into a vacant pew. Maggie twisted the handle of her purse then put it beside her on the bench as she knelt down making the sign of the cross.

Two women in cotton capris and matching golf shirts stood in line waiting to make their confession. Three older men and a young teenage girl knelt in other pews, hands folded and heads bent in prayer.

"I don't like him," said Maggie reaching up to touch the cross at her neck.

"You don't like who?" Lizzie asked.

"Him, that priest. Is there anyone else?" Maggie hissed.

"No. If you want to go to confession, he's it," said Lizzie in her most authoritative whisper. What did she have to confess anyway? This is ridiculous she thought.

"Take me home. I don't like him. I don't trust him. We don't know who he'll talk to."

"Mom, he isn't going to talk to anyone. He's a priest," Lizzie tried again to convince her to stay.

Maggie picked up her purse, moved out of the pew and walked down the aisle, away from the altar, to the front of the church. She stopped suddenly as if someone was in her path. Turning around she looked at the imposing marble alter with the massive crucifix suspended above and the dazzling dancing colors formed by the sun shining through the stain glass windows. Maggie grabbed hold of the end of the long wooden pew with her left hand, knelt down on one knee and made the sign of the cross with her right. Her lips moved in a silent prayer.

"Lizzie, hurry up," came the loud whisper as she got to her feet and moved once more toward the door.

* * *

Back home they sat by the pool. There was a slight breeze blowing and the silence was companionable. Again, Maggie did not seem to remember the unsettling events of the day.

Lizzie got up and announced "Dinner will be salad with grilled chicken. Plus that loaf of fresh bread we bought at the sale today. I've got pie for desert or zucchini bread."

"I'll help," said Maggie as she got up and headed across the deck.

Maggie took a stick of butter from the refrigerator, removed the wrapper and placed it in a dish to soften on the counter.

"We gave up a lot during the war. The hardest for me was butter. I love butter on my bread. And sugar for my tea," Maggie said leaning against the counter.

"Really, what else did you have to live without? " Lizzie asked as she reached for a pan from the lower cabinet.

"Oh, I don't remember now. Butter, sugar and my family."

Lizzie straightened to stare at her mother. "Your family? I thought your family died before the war even started."

"Oh no dear, I'm not sure what become of them. It wasn't safe to find them. Then my Sam found me. My Sam."

Lizzie started to ask another question but saw agitation on Maggie's face. "It's okay. Can you help me with the dinner? I need napkins and silverware, please."

* * *

Dan arrived home late, after Maggie had gone to sleep. Lizzie was reading in bed, propped up with extra pillows, trying to stay awake.

"Dan, she kept asking about you. All day long. Where were you from? Were you married before? Didn't you have a family back home? When did you start going by Dan when you were always called Danny? It was the strangest thing. I tried to tell her, to explain that we had been together for years, you had not been called Danny since you were about four or five years old and your family was here in Florida. Finally this evening we went round and round again. It went on for ten or fifteen minutes then she cocked her head to the right, got this odd look on her face and said, 'never mind. It's best. Danny's right not to say anything.' After that she finished her tea and went off to bed."

"Don't worry. It's just the illness. I may remind her of some old boyfriend," Dan laughed and headed for the shower. "Too many sand traps today."

Chapter 10

Ian offered to take Maggie home after her two weeks with Lizzie. They were both quiet on the ride down Gulf Blvd. Maggie looked out at the palm trees and tall condos blocking the view of the Gulf.

When they were two blocks from her condo Maggie turned to him and in her most polite voice said, "Thank you young man, I appreciate the ride. Would you mind calling my husband Sam? He may not be home and I seem to have misplaced my keys. I have his number somewhere here in my purse."

Ian could not keep the alarm from his voice. "Quit joking Mom. What are you talking about? I have your keys."

A disconnected look was on Maggie's face for a few moments then disappeared to be replaced by a shy smile. "Of course you have the keys, dear. Let's go inside and have a nice cup of tea."

Once inside Ian sat at the kitchen table while Maggie went about filling the kettle for tea and pulling cups from the cupboard. Ian looked out the window at the bright blue sky over the Gulf. People of all ages were splashing in the water or lying on brightly colored beach towels in the sand. He watched two young boys throw a Frisbee back and forth and thought of the times his father played with his kids in the waves. He tried to fill the time with idle chatter about his golfing buddies, many whom she knew, when he noticed she had picked up a tea towel and was twisting it with shaking hands.

"Here Mom, let me do this. Sit down. I'll have the tea on the table in a minute. Lizzie sent along a bag of her homemade cookies. Let's have some now." Ian made the tea and they drank the strong bracing brew in silence. Finally he asked, "How are you doing?"

"Fine."

Frustrated by her response, he protested, "You're not fine. We need to talk about what's going to happen."

"Nothing is going to happen," Maggie said quietly. "I'm home and I want to stay at home. I don't want to be a bother. You all have enough to take care of, busy with work and family. Besides, my friend is just down the hall. I have lots of friends."

"Mom," Ian started.

Before he could continue, Maggie said "I get a bit confused, a bit forgetful. I'm fine. It happens to everyone my age. One day it will happen to you, too."

"It's not just the forgetting someone's name. We need to talk about this. We love you. You are never a bother to any of us. Please, we just want to help," he pleaded.

The concern showed in his soft blue eyes, those blue eyes so like Sam's, "Sam, where is he?" Maggie asked in almost a whisper.

"What'd you say Mom?" asked Ian

Before she could answer Maggie realized her beloved Sam was gone. It struck her with an intensity she had not felt for a long time. The anger at being left alone became focused on her son.

"I'm fine," she said loudly, slamming her cup on the table, spilling the tea and staining the yellow placemats. "Now look what you did. Clean this up quickly before the tea spreads all over."

Ian felt the shock of her anger like stepping into an ice cold shower. He jumped to his feet to grab paper towels to sop up the tea. She was strong, intelligent, still charming and flirty. What was happening to her now was unbelievable. He knew the doctor and Lizzie were right. He had seen signs that something was wrong but dismissed them because he didn't want to deal with this situation. Alzheimer's. Dementia. It didn't matter what you called it, it was not pretty. He had friends whose parents or grandparents where going through the same thing. Personality changes happen. Who wouldn't go from being a nice guy to a cranky old man if you knew you were losing your mind? The memory loss is devastating. Not knowing your spouse, your kids. Forgetting years and years of your life as if they never happened. He had to stop thinking about this. Talk about something else.

"It's all cleaned up. Let me get us both another cup of tea. We'll have a few more of Lizzie's cookies. She's a great baker but her cookies are not as good as yours."

With those calming words Maggie looked up at her son with a warm smile. "Thank you darling. A cup of tea would be lovely."

Chapter 11

After Ian left Maggie he called Lizzie and Kevin to meet him for coffee after work at the Little Family Diner. The local restaurant had been a favorite of theirs for Saturday morning breakfasts when they felt the need to get away and whine about mom or dad, their families or work. The three of them were close, bound together by need. Their parents, so singularly in love with each other, often kept the kids at arm's length or so they felt. It was almost as if they were afraid to get too close. When she was young, Lizzie complained their parents only had kids to help with the chores.

There was an unspoken pact; whatever was talked about at the Diner was never discussed with anyone else. Not spouses or friends and mostly not the parents. It had been helpful to have this safe outlet when Ian was thinking about a divorce. He needed to say out loud he was angry with Rose for not being a better wife. He needed to have someone hear his words and offer support. His brother and sister could not repair his marriage but they could listen and because they knew him so well, provide some insight. Somehow advice given by any one of the three over a cup of hot black coffee was reasonable and more often than not followed.

Kevin suggested Ian go home and treat Rose like he did when they first met. "Look for the qualities that made you want her in the first place," he told him.

Ian had snickered, "Her boobs were quite fascinating when I was 18 but have lost some of their intrigue after 35 years."

The talk had continued but on a lighter note. Ian

understood the meaning of his younger brother's advice. He had gone home and was nicer to Rose. It worked. They might never have what his parents had. They might never be so crazy in love like Lizzie and Dan. Even after 30 years of marriage people thought Lizzie and Dan were newlyweds. But, Ian and Rose were headed in the right direction.

Lizzie waited at their table at the back of the restaurant. She loved this old place with its tin ceilings and raw red brick walls. The scarred wooden tables were surrounded by hand painted mix and match chairs with big comfy seats and high slatted backs. There was a line of people standing on the wide plank floor in front of the glass display counter filled with trays of fresh baked pies, cookies and cakes. Large glass jars held biscotti; chocolate dipped chocolate biscotti, one of her favorite treats. She had refrained from ordering any when she asked for a pot of coffee and three cups. Maybe later. Lizzie looked at the oversize black and white clock on the wall behind the register ticking away the minutes. She wondered how this thing with Maggie was going to change their lives.

"What are we going to do?" Lizzie asked when Ian and Kevin sat down. "She's confused. She doesn't know what she's doing. You should have seen her this morning before you picked her up."

Ian, not one to sugar coat, flatly stated "Mom has Alzheimer's. I'm sure it is the early stages."

"They could be wrong," said Kevin. "She's just old. All old people get confused. She's grieving, not thinking."

Lizzie knew it was more than grief and old age. "The confusion. We've all seen it. I wanted to write it off to grief over loosing Dad. We all do. But...but there is something more. She was crazy today. One minute scared, the next confident and laughing."

Lizzie desperately wanted to believe there was no real problem, but these private thoughts had been put into words and spoken out loud by her doctor, given a name: Alzheimer's.

That diagnosis could not be unsaid. There were signs, lost looks, confusion over simple tasks, not remembering names. She looked the same but was slightly off kilter. As much as she wanted to deny it she knew it was the truth.

"It's age and grief," Kevin stated but not as firmly as before. "Age and grief."

"It doesn't matter what it is. We need to do something," said Lizzie knowing her brothers would struggle with that label until the end.

The three kids were faced with a difficult decision. One they had hoped never to make. Or if they did, Maggie would have been a part of. Now they needed to decide the future for her.

"We have to take her car away," said Lizzie picking up her coffee and looking at both her brothers, she tried not to smile. She knew their reaction as surely as she knew what her mother's would be.

"Not me. No sir, not me," Kevin was defiant. Pointing at Lizzie and Ian he stated firmly, "You be the bad guys. You take her car. Not me. She'll hate whoever even brings it up."

"Kevin, don't be stupid. She knows she can't drive forever. We've talked about other friends of hers who have given up their cars," Ian said as he sipped his coffee and motioned for Angela, their waitress.

"Well if it's no big deal, you be the one," laughed Lizzie "I'll have the chocolate dipped chocolate biscotti please and more coffee. I shouldn't be having this but chocolate is a necessity now."

Both men ordered the extra-large chocolate chip cookies, then smiling Kevin said, "Don't tell Becca. She wants me to cut down on sugar."

"Back to the car issue," Ian stated.

"She'll never agree," said Kevin shaking his head.

"She has to," Ian declared calmly as if by saying the words aloud it became fact. "Moving on. We have to do this thing in stages. She can still live alone during the week and stay with one of us on the weekends. We can check on her during the day. Between us and the Gee Kids we should be able to set up a schedule."

"Oh come on you guys. That sounds like a babysitting schedule. She'll never go for it," said Lizzie. "Besides we haven't told the Gee Kids."

"I don't think it is necessary to announce she has Alzheimer's to them," Ian said, sipping his coffee. "All they need to know is she is getting older and needs a little more attention now that Grandpa Sam is gone."

"If that's how you want to handle it, fine," Lizzie grumbled, glaring at her older brother.

Kevin piped up, "Why do they need to know? It's such a horrible thing to say."

"I said fine. Let's just move on," Lizzie said, frustration settling in the lines around her mouth.

"Let's talk about this. If we give her the choice of this schedule or living full time with one of us I think she'll agree," said Ian.

"One of us?" Lizzie astonishment was clearly visible on her face. "You both know she won't stay long term with either of you. I'm not saying we won't take her but don't make it sound like there is any chance of her moving in with you."

Her anger was rising until she looked at her two grinning brothers. She knew they would have her but also knew it wasn't their call. Moms didn't live with their married sons. As if reading Lizzie's mind the boys recited in a singsong voice, a saying Maggie had repeated multiple times since they had gotten married, "A son is a son until he takes a wife, a daughter is a daughter all of her life."

They spent the next hour creating a plan and a rough schedule which would be refined as they weeks progressed. The first step was a sit down with their mom. It would not help for the three of them to descend on Maggie and tell her they were taking over her life. Lizzie knew it would be best for her to be the one to lay it all out. Everything except the issue of the car. She would leave that to Ian.

* * *

The next day was Friday and Lizzie had taken the afternoon off from work to visit with her mom at the condo. She arrived at one o'clock with a bag of cookies and a smile. Her carefully worded explanation was met with stony silence. Lizzie busied herself in the kitchen making tea and setting the cookies on a plate.

"I'm fine now and I won't be alone," Maggie said. "My friend is coming over for a movie night. We're going to make a big bowl of popcorn and watch that movie about the war."

"What movie?" asked Lizzie.

"You know the one about the war and the nurses. It's a sad movie but good."

"Pearl Harbor? That is a sad movie. Are you sure you want to watch it?"

"It's our time Lizzie. It's a story about people we know. My friend will take me to Mass on Sunday. I'll be fine."

Lizzie tried again, "I know you are independent and are okay living here by yourself for a while, but..."

"But nothing," Maggie interrupted shaking the cookie in her hand at Lizzie. "I can make my own decisions. I have friends. This is my home and I'm staying here. That's final."

Chapter 12

It was still dark outside. The house phone rang as Lizzie walked through the front door from grabbing the Monday morning paper off the lawn. The plastic wrapper was wet with dew and she tried unsuccessfully not to drip it on the floor. Who could be calling at 5:30 she thought. She knew not to panic. Their kids called Dan's cell if there was a problem and everyone else called her cell. The house phone was usually someone with something to sell or a wrong number. Just in case she grabbed the portable off the base as she walked past the sofa table on her way to the kitchen.

"Hello."

"Hello. Is this Lizzie Callahan?"

"Yes. Can I help you?" she said stifling a yawn.

"Yes. This is Sergeant Macklin from the Largo Police Department."

"Oh my God. What's wrong?" said Lizzie, now fully awake.

"Ms. Callahan are you related to a Margaret Murphy?"

"Oh my God," she said slumping against the counter.

Just then Dan walked into the kitchen. "What's the matter?" Her large green eyes were wild with alarm and the hand holding the phone to her ear was shaking. "Here, Lizzie, let me have the phone," Dan said as he steered her towards a bar stool.

"Hello. This is Dan Callahan. Who am I speaking with?"

"This is Sergeant Macklin from the Largo Police Department. Do you know Margaret Murphy?"

"She's my mother-in-law. What's wrong?" Dan's arm was around Lizzie's shoulder and she leaned into his chest.

"She was in a car accident. She's been taken to the hospital for observation. There were a few cuts and bruises from the air bag but she was conscious and talking. She asked me to contact her sister Bridget but I didn't find a number for Bridget in her purse or phone. The ICE number in her cell is Lizzie Callahan."

"Lizzie's my wife. Where are they taking Maggie?" Holding her tight and rubbing her back he whispered, "She's alright."

"She'll be at Largo Medical. The accident happened near the hospital. Single car accident. She hit a tree. We're not sure what happened but it seems she was going east on West Bay Drive when she lost control of the car, crossed over the five lanes of traffic and hit a tree in the parking lot of the Beautiful Bouquet Flower Shop then went through the plate glass window. There is a lot of damage but no one was hurt. This early there aren't a lot of people on the streets and no one was in the store."

"We'll be right over. Thanks Sergeant," Dan said then disconnected the call and placed the phone on the countertop. Lizzie didn't speak, just clung to him, her checks and his shirt wet with tears. She started to shiver, wrapping her arms around her chest.

"Lizzie, Maggie's fine." He spoke softly as he rocked her a bit and ran his hand through her hair. "Let me make a pot of coffee while you get ready. Take a quick shower and we'll leave in a few minutes. I'll call Ian and Kevin. Go on now." He kissed the top of her head then tilted her chin up to kiss her softly on the lips.

Like a frightened child, Lizzie got up and wrapped her arms around Dan. She stayed there for a long time, not wanting to go on with the day, not wanting to leave the protection of his arms, not wanting to face whatever was happening. Finally, knowing she had no choice, she stepped back from his embrace, kissed him, and moved quickly to the bedroom.

She could smell the coffee brewing as she stepped out of the shower. Before she was dried off Dan walked into the spacious master bath holding two mugs. Wrapping herself in the large white towel she leaned against the green marble counter. He set the coffee down and put both hands on Lizzie's shoulders.

"Look at me Lizzie."

"I can't lose her too, Dan. I can't lose Mom too," Lizzie declared.

"She's alright. The police would have shown up at the door, not called on the phone if it was bad," Dan said, gently touching her cheek.

"What was she doing out at this time of morning? Where was she going? Why was she driving on West Bay at five o'clock in the morning?" she asked her voice sharp with anxiety.

"We'll find out when we see her. Drink your coffee and get ready. We can be at the hospital in half an hour. I've called your brothers. They'll meet us there."

Dan drove so he could go to work after checking on Maggie. He knew one of her brothers would give Lizzie a ride back home or he would pick her up later. If she was admitted to the hospital Lizzie would be staying, too.

"She agreed not to drive. I should have taken the keys. Why didn't I do that? So what if she was upset," Lizzie argued.

"Stop it," Dan demanded, hands tightening on the steering wheel.

"Dan, it's true. She might have killed someone or herself. When Ian talked to her yesterday she agreed to give the car to Timmy. He will be 16 in July. Oh, Grand Maggie was gracious and kind when she agreed," said Lizzie with a nasty edge. "I didn't think she would drive again Dan. How stupid am I?" Slapping her hands on her thighs she said "Oh my God. What did Ian and Kevin say? They must be livid."

"Lizzie, stop it. Ian believed her. We all did. Why wouldn't you?" Dan said turning to look at her. "They not going to blame you and you're not helping by blaming yourself. It's only been a few weeks since we found out about the Alzheimer's. No one knows what to expect. Everyone agreed it was safe for her to go home for a few days by herself. She seemed fine. Who knew she would get up in the middle of the night and go for a drive?"

Chapter 13

Ian drove into the Hampton Plaza parking lot expecting to see minor damage to the front of the flower shop.

"Good God," he said climbing out of his BMW to survey the destruction. The entire front window was gone. A riot of colorful flower petals, green leaves and broken stems carpeted the walkway and floor. Shards of glass glinted in the early morning sunlight like fairy lights. Maggie's car had gone over the curb, glanced off the massive oak tree then smashed into the large plate glass window, mangling the chrome and glass counter as she continued through, finally ramming the whole mess into the fresh flower cooler at the back.

The police were still on the scene. Ian walked over to the nearest policeman who held up his hand in a stop right there motion. "Sir, you need to stay back," he said.

"I'm Ian Murphy. My mother was involved in this accident."

"You still need to stay back. We're not sure how much damage the building sustained."

"No one was in there?" Ian asked, fear etched on his face.

"No sir. The owner and employees had not come to work yet."

Ian raked his hand over his hair and took two steps back as he surveyed the carnage.

"Your mother was taken to Largo Medical Hospital. She was conscious and talking though she seemed confused. We have her purse, cell phone and identification." Pointing to a tall policeman over by the crumpled and crushed vehicle he continued, "I'm sure Sergeant Markham would like to ask you a few questions."

"How did this happen?" Ian asked shaking his head. "How was she not killed?"

"I can't answer that one sir." he said as they walked over to the officer in charge.

After introductions Sergeant Markham asked, "Can you tell me about you mother? Does she have any health issues?"

Automatically Ian replied, "No, not really."

"Did anything happen recently?"

"Ah...my dad died in April," Ian said turning again to look into the mess of the flower shop.

"I'm sorry for your loss." Officer Markham said sounding sincere. "Was she distraught?"

"Well yes, but she was okay," Ian replied but not with the same conviction he would have answered that question only yesterday.

"Do you know where she was going at that early hour?"

"No idea," Ian said wiping the sweat from his forehead. It wasn't quite seven and already the temperature was over eighty degrees.

"Do you know a Bridget Malone?"

"No. Malone is my mom's maiden name but her family is long dead in Ireland."

"Your mother was insistent she was meeting Bridget Malone. Said she had seen her a few days ago."

"Yes, well, there was an EMT named Bridget that my mom thought she knew," Ian said shoving his hand in his pocket, jingling the change there.

"An EMT?" asked Officer Markham, eyebrows rising slightly.

"Yes. She fell recently and we had to call an ambulance. This EMT was able to settle her down. Her name was Bridget. I don't know her last name. I'm on my way the hospital now. I'll talk to her."

"Someone will be over to interview your mother later this morning."

Ian reached out to shake the officer's hand. "Thank you for everything. I'm sorry for all this," he said motioning to the ravaged tree and the devastated store.

"We're glad you mom is unhurt. She was lucky, this time," Officer Markham said.

Ian walked slowly back to his car. Opening the door he surveyed the damage once more before climbing in. "Thank God she's okay and no one else was hurt," he said aloud.

Chapter 14

Maggie spent most of the day in the ER and was finally admitted to the hospital in late afternoon for observation. If everything was okay in the morning she would be released, if she agreed to go home with one of her children. She seemed less confused as the orderlies and nurse settled her in the hospital bed. Lizzie said she was staying and Maggie did not object.

"Where will you sleep?" Maggie asked looking around the private room.

"Right here in this chair," said Lizzie, indicating a faux leather padded recliner. It didn't look comfortable but it was better than the molded plastic chair off in the corner.

"You will not," Maggie said pointing a finger at Lizzie. "I can move over and you can sleep here in the bed with me."

"No, there isn't enough room. Besides you have those IV's in your arm," Lizzie reminded her. Smiling she continued, "I don't want to get tangled up in them."

Distracted now Maggie raised her left hand. The IV needle and a curl of tubing were held firmly in place with surgical tape. The rest of the tubing snaked down her arm and over the sheets. "Yes, what are these for?" she asked frowning.

"Just some medications and fluids."

"I just took a pill and a drink of water. I don't need this," she said rattling her arm and hitting her hand on the side rail that had been raised to keep her in bed.

"Oww, that hurt," yelped Maggie looking down at her hand. She wrinkled her face and Lizzie thought she was going to cry.

"It's okay Mom," Lizzie soothed rushing to the side of the bed. "Here, let me see." The needle didn't seem to be dislodged and there was no blood but she pushed the button on the control pad to call the nurse. Holding her hand Lizzie said, "They want to you to leave it in just till tomorrow. The nurse will take it out in the morning. I've called her to come check it, make sure you didn't hurt yourself."

"I did hurt myself," Maggie said firmly.

Just then a tall nurse dressed in blue scrubs came into the room. "I'm Jane, your nurse for this evening. How are you doing Margaret?" she asked.

"Who's Margaret?" Maggie asked looking around her private room.

"She goes by Maggie," said Lizzie.

"Well Maggie, I see here you were in a car accident. You were lucky. No broken bones, just a few cuts and bruises."

"Yes," said Lizzie. "Her Guardian Angel must have been watching over her."

Having forgotten the IV in her hand, Maggie looked up at Jane and stated "She can't sleep in a chair. She can sleep with me but she won't. She can't sleep in the chair."

"I'll see about getting a cot in here for her. Is this your daughter?" Jane asked.

Maggie looked at Lizzie in confusion then turned to Jane. "She's going to stay with me. She needs a bed to sleep in."

"Lizzie, I'm her daughter, Lizzie," she said, a flush rising to her cheeks. Turning towards the door she asked "Is it okay if I step out of the room for a few minutes? Maybe get a cup of coffee?"

"Sure honey. We'll be just fine here. I need to get her vitals. You can go to the kitchen area down the hall. Fresh coffee all the time. Help yourself," said Jane with a sympathetic smile.

Standing out in the hall Lizzie took a deep breath and

leaned against the wall. She could hear Jane and Maggie talking. Jane, her kind voice soothing and Maggie, agitated and demanding an extra bed in the room. Pulling her phone from her pocket she called Dan.

"She doesn't know me Dan," said Lizzie in a hushed tone rubbing the back of her neck. The headache that had been lingering at the base of her skull was now pounding with full hurricane force on her brain.

"Maybe not this minute but she will again. It comes and goes Lizzie. You know that. It will be okay," Dan said patiently. "I'll be by shortly. Had to finish up some paperwork after a conference call. Want me to bring you something to eat?"

"Sure, we can eat together in the room. Maggie's already had her dinner. She didn't eat much, just soup and crackers. A little pudding. "

"Need anything else?" Dan asked.

"Yes, some aspirin. My head is pounding." she said reaching up to massage her neck then smiled wryly. "Funny, this is a hospital and I can't get an aspirin because I'm not a patient. I borrowed Kevin's car while he visited with Mom and went home to grab a few things but forgot aspirin. Didn't make a list to check off. She will be released tomorrow. They're going to get a cot for me to sleep on. I should get back into the room. The nurse is done in there."

"See you soon. I love you," Dan said.

"I love you, too," she murmured.

"Are you okay?" asked the nurse as she came through the door from Maggie's room.

"Yes. I'm fine," said Lizzie even though she wasn't. "It's upsetting when she doesn't know me."

"Of course it is. But she does know you. Maybe not that you're her daughter, but she knows you love her and she is safe with you. That's real important."

"Yes it is," said Lizzie sighing. "It's just that I never know who she thinks I am."

* * *

The noise in the hospital though hushed kept Lizzie awake. Maggie dozed and woke often with a start, not knowing where she was. Lizzie comforted her as best she could. Finally the light peeked through the blinds as the sun rose. The noise in the hallway increased. Lizzie got off the cot and went to the bathroom to splash water on her face and brush her teeth. Looking in the mirror she saw the dark circles under her eyes that makeup wouldn't fix it. This day would be long. Even though Maggie was to be released this morning it would not be until hours from now, possibly not until afternoon. Hospitals worked on a time of their own making. When someone said in a few minutes it could be half an hour or longer.

As Lizzie returned to the bedroom Maggie was struggling to wake up. "Where am I?" she asked.

"In the hospital. You had a car accident yesterday and they wanted to keep you over night to make sure everything was okay."

"What car accident?" she asked, eyes wide furtively looking around the room. "Where? Who was driving?"

"You were. You ran into a tree and then into a flower shop."

"I did no such thing. I don't remember an accident," Maggie stated indignantly trying to sit up. "What is all this?" she asked waving her left arm at Lizzie.

"The IV. The nurse will take it out soon. The doctor will be here shortly to release you then I can take you home."

"I don't remember an accident," Maggie repeated, softly this time. Looking down at her hands she began to gently twist the sheet.

"It's okay. We'll be out of here soon. They will bring you tea and breakfast in bed. Then it won't be long." Lizzie said in a reassuring voice. "Everything is fine."

Just then the orderly arrived with the breakfast tray. He

raised the top of her bed so she was sitting up. Lizzie fluffed the pillows at her back and went about uncovering the meal and making the tea.

"Looks good Mom. Scrambled eggs. Even jelly for your toast."

"Where's yours?" Maggie asked.

"I'll get something later. Here you eat."

"No dear, you have some too," Maggie said offering a piece of toast.

"I'm fine. I'll just get a cup of coffee from the nurse's station," Lizzie said.

"They won't mind?" Maggie asked bring the steaming cup to her lips.

"No. I'll be right back. You eat now," Lizzie said as she headed out the door. Walking to the small kitchen down the hall she asked if she could get a cup of coffee.

"Help yourself," said the young nurse getting juice from the under counter refrigerator.

"Thanks. I can put up with almost anything as long as I have my coffee," Lizzie replied reaching for a Styrofoam cup.

"I hear that," the nurse answered with a smile.

Back in the room Lizzie settled in the chair, sipped her coffee and watched her mom eat. She seemed to manage even with the IV in her hand. When she was done she lay back on the pillow and closed her eyes. Her lips were moving but no words could be heard. Slowly she opened her eyes and said, "I need to go to confession."

"Not now. I'll take you later."

"When?"

"On Saturday. That's when they hear confessions," Lizzie replied.

"Okay dear."

* * *

Hours later the doctor arrived and after a few minutes reading her chart and checking her over agreed to release Maggie if she would go to her daughter's home.

"We want to have someone with you for a while," said Dr. Harvey.

"I'll stay with her for a few days," Maggie said pointing to Lizzie.

"That works. Then you need to follow-up with your regular physician in a couple of days. I'm sending you home with a prescription for a mild pain medication. Only take it if necessary," he said looking at Lizzie who nodded.

* * *

Ian took the afternoon off work to drive Maggie from the hospital. Lizzie left earlier to get ready for her.

"I don't know why everyone is making such a fuss," Maggie said as Ian tried to buckle her seat belt. She slapped his hand away and said "I can do that myself.'

"I know you can, I'm just trying to help."

"You can help by taking me home," demanded Maggie.

"You're going to Lizzie's for a bit," Ian replied trying not to provoke a fight.

"I am not," Maggie stated firmly clasping her hands together and sitting rigidly in the seat.

"Just for a few days. The doc would only release you if you agreed to stay with someone. You did agree to that you know."

"Of course I did. How else would I have gotten out? Now take me home," said Maggie as she batted at Ian with her left hand.

"Stop that," Ian yelled. "You're going to Lizzie's for a few days."

The hopelessness of the situation settled around Maggie

like a blanket as her shoulders slumped and she lowered her head. Absently she reached for the cross at her throat. Ian drove the rest of the way to Lizzie's house in silence. Glancing over at his mother he noticed she closed her eyes and seemed to sleep. He wasn't sure how things would play out once they arrived but he would deal with it then.

As he put the car in park, Maggie opened her eyes and said, "Where are we?" her voice tight with alarm.

"I told you I was bringing you to Lizzie's. Here's Dan now."

At the mention of Dan's name Maggie brightened. She patted her hair and turned to smile at Ian. "Thank you for bring me here, darling. I have wanted to see Danny for such a long time."

"Really?" said Ian surprised and thankful his mother was not angry.

Dan opened the door and offered Maggie his hand to assist her out of the car.

"Danny you are so kind. I have been looking forward to seeing you. What a lovely home you have. And, on the water too," she said with a cheerful smile.

An amused Dan looked over at Ian coming around the car.

"Don't ask me. I picked her up at the hospital and she was not happy when I told her I was bringing her to Lizzie's." Ian waved his arm toward the house and said sarcastically, "I guess I should have said Danny's."

"Come on Maggie," said Dan taking her arm and leading her to the front door.

Lizzie had the kettle on and was making tea when Maggie and Dan walked into the kitchen.

"Look who's here for a visit," said Dan smiling.

"Hi Mom. Have a seat in the family room and I'll bring you some tea," said Lizzie.

Ignoring Lizzie, Maggie said, "Oh Danny, this is lovely."

She settled herself in the chair by the window. "What a lovely view. I do so like looking at the water. Is that your boat?"

"Yes it is, the Lizzie Lou. Named after your beautiful daughter. Maybe we can take it out later," he said.

Ian and Lizzie stood in the kitchen listening to the exchange. "What is going on?" quizzed Lizzie.

"No idea," said Ian. "She was hopping mad I was bringing her here until she saw Dan."

"What?' asked Lizzie turning to look at him.

"Don't know. Just that she calmed down and was happy to see Dan," said Ian with a shrug.

"Whatever works," sighed Lizzie. "She always liked Dan." She grabbed a tray and loaded it with cups of tea, coffee and a plate of cookies. The four of them sat in the living room talking about the weather, boating and how the Tampa Bay Rays were doing. Maggie kept watching Dan with a shy smile on her face. No one mentioned that Maggie would be staying. When Ian got up to leave he walked over to his mother to give her a kiss.

"I'll come by later in the week Mom."

"That would be lovely, dear," said Maggie reaching up to pat his cheek.

Chapter 15

Dan asked Maggie to sit out on the deck with him for a drink Wednesday, the one evening he made it home before eight o'clock. "I picked up a loaf of that fresh olive bread Lizzie loves to go with the roast pork she's made. She's making a salad now. I have a favor to ask."

He helped Maggie out the back door. She did not protest that she was able to walk by herself as she did when Ian or Kevin tried to assist her. She took his offered arm and leaned into him, just a little.

"It's nice to have a gentleman about," she murmured. Dan walked her to the deck chair and helped her settle in.

Lizzie watched but couldn't hear their conversations as she stood smiling at the kitchen counter. She was grateful for Dan. They had been through some difficult times. Both twins breaking their arms just days apart when they were ten. Opening her own real estate office and struggling through the first few years as she built up her client list and added agents. Her cancer scare when the annual mammogram showed a lump which thankfully was benign. And then the car accident that killed Dan's favorite uncle. A drunk driver had run a red light plowing into the driver's side, killing him instantly. No matter the personal or financial problems they always managed to come stronger because they loved each other. This situation with Maggie would add tremendous stress to the entire family. Seeing the two of them chatting and laughing on the deck made her appreciate Dan even more. She knew they would be fine in the end regardless of the troubles coming their way.

"How about it Maggie? Want a quick ride around the

neighborhood?" asked Dan pointing towards the boat gently bobbing at the dock.

She giggled like a school girl and even blushed a bit. "No. No. Don't want to mess up my hair," she said reaching up to pat her short grey curls.

He smiled and took the seat beside her. "Maggie, I'll be working late quite often this summer. I hate to leave Lizzie home alone. I know she is fine by herself but she does spend too much time worrying about our kids and Ian and Kevin's kids. You know how she is," Dan smiled and pointed towards the kitchen where Lizzie's stood by the sliding glass door. "Anyway, I know you have your own life and we shouldn't impose after all you've done but.... would you stay with us this summer?" He ran his fingers through his dark blonde hair and glanced over at Maggie trying to gauge her reaction. She sat with her hands clasped loosely in her lap and the barest beginning of a smile on her lips. Lips that were perfectly lined and colored. She was never seen without lipstick.

"I haven't said anything to Lizzie," Dan rushed on. "She doesn't know I'm talking to you...but she has mentioned several times that she wanted you to stay for a while." This little white lie was devised by Dan and Lizzie late the night before. They realized Maggie responded better to Dan, though they had no idea why. If he asked her to stay and she agreed, it would be easier in the future to remind her of the promise to Dan.

Before Maggie could say a word, he went on. "The kids are busy with their lives. She has friends too but what she would really love is to have more time with you. I know it's asking a lot Maggie. Just until Labor Day. We'll have our big family party and then when it settles down in September you can go back to your condo. What do you say?" His blue eyes were intent on Maggie's face as he reached out to pat her hand.

"Yes Danny, of course I will. I love being here with you," Maggie said, her face alight with affection as she leaned over to kiss his cheek.

Dan was pleased Maggie had agreed so quickly that he failed to notice she called him Danny. He was called Danny for the first four years of his life. One rainy Sunday afternoon a few weeks after he turned four, when he and his parents sat at the dining room table putting together a one hundred piece picture puzzle of teddy bears of all colors and sizes he announced he would no longer be Danny. "That's a baby name. I'm no baby. I'm Dan." His parents gave in to the desires of their only child, so he was Dan from that day forward.

Chapter 16

Some days Maggie seemed not to know where she was. She was not in Lizzie's home or if she was, Lizzie was not her daughter. Often she thought she was in Ireland before the war. She spoke in snatches about people and places no one had ever heard about. Lizzie and her brothers knew very little of their mother's childhood. She survived, as she often said "A terrible time. Terrible, terrible time."

In the past she refused to talk about her childhood, repeating the same story when ever asked, "I was orphaned just before the war. They all died in a fire. I had no one. I went to England to live with a spinster aunt and help with the war effort in a shoe factory, met your father, my Sam, and came to America. Everything good and lovely happened after that."

Maggie would ask Lizzie if she had seen Mary or Betty or some other unknown person. At first she responded with a sigh and an explanation as to where they were, who she was and how she didn't know any of these people. But after a suggestion by Dan to forget about reality for a while and listen to the stories, Lizzie found it easier to go with the moment.

Ian and Kevin stopped in the kitchen for coffee with Lizzie after coming back from taking Maggie to Mass one Saturday morning in late June. The kitchen was still warm and the delicious scent of sugar and peanut butter wafted through.

"I'm going to lay down for a bit," said Maggie after she finished her tea. "I'll see you all later."

The three remained sitting at the breakfast bar, spinning on their stools and wolfing down the warm peanut butter cookies placed before them. Lizzie had gotten up early but could not sit still and read the paper. She needed to move about. Her brothers loved her cookies so she could stay busy and make them happy.

"She's moving away from us," said Kevin. "She never calls me by my name. I know she always said dear or honey but she did use my name sometimes. Not now. Even when I hug her I don't think it's her hugging me back."

Both men were struggling and Lizzie knew they had to come to terms with this disease and what it was doing to their mother it in on their own but she wanted to help. "Just try to stay with her no matter where she is," Lizzie suggested after pouring more coffee for all three of them. "I don't correct her when she thinks I'm her friend from Ireland. I listen to her stories. It's interesting to hear about the butcher shop in town with the meat in the window or the playing with the neighbor's kittens."

"I don't know how to do that. I want to correct her. Say I'm your son Kevin when she looks at me in that odd way. I want it to be like it was," he said grabbing another cookie and sighing. "I'll try Lizzie but, I don't know."

"I get what you're saying Lizzie but maybe if we all work to keep her in the present it will help her stay here in the present. We have to help her remember who we are and where she is," Ian said.

Laughing, Lizzie said "Do you win that argument with her?"

"It's not a matter of winning or losing. It's helping. It's trying to stay on course, in reality. Not letting her drift off."

"You guys can do what you think is best. I have her here and I am trying to get through the days with as little turmoil as possible. If letting her think she is in Ireland makes for a more enjoyable day, well guess what? We're in Ireland," Lizzie said getting up to add more cookies to the plate. "What about the Fourth of July? We can do a cook out here."

"Do you think she'll be okay with all the Gee-kids running about? Will it be too much?" asked Ian as he held tightly to his cup and stared out the window watching the pelicans soar and dive for their lunch. "We still haven't told them what's wrong with her."

Ignoring his last statement, she said, "How 'bout we have everyone here early, cook burgers and dogs and then send them on their way. The kids will understand. They want to see Grand Maggie but also have stuff to do. You remember what it was like with young kids. They can go watch fireworks on their own. You guys can stay here or go home. Whatever works." It seemed Lizzie was learning to manage the details of this new life with less stress than she had imagined. Dan's advice to live in the moment helped.

Awhile after the brothers had left Maggie came into the kitchen. Her hair was mussed and her glasses askew. She looked around the kitchen and family room, clutching at the cross at her neck. "Where is everyone?" she asked.

"Kevin and Ian went home. Dan has gone golfing. It's just me here," said Lizzie.

"I heard voices," said Maggie. "Who was here?"

"Just Ian and Kevin. They brought you back from Mass and stayed for coffee. You went to lie down."

"What were you talking about?" Maggie asked her eyes scanning the rooms.

"Just things, nothing special."

"Do they know what happened to Bridget?" Maggie asked.

"No Mom," said Lizzie. "No one knows what happened to Bridget."

"I saw her not long ago. Did you tell her not to come back? I know it's not safe but maybe now it's okay," said Maggie, reaching out to touch Lizzie's arm. "I really want to see her again."

"No I didn't tell her not to come back. I don't know where she is. Maybe she'll stop by later. Do you want a cup of tea?" Lizzie replied but thought maybe I can get that redhead back here someday to talk to her. Maybe that would help. She realized it was a foolish idea and didn't want to bring anyone else into their little drama. "Here, have a cookie while I make your tea."

Ignoring Lizzie Maggie said "Bridget would have come here only if it was safe."

"Then it must be safe," said Lizzie placing the cup of steaming tea with cream and sugar in front of her mother. See any money in there today?"

Looking into the tea cup Maggie saw the bubbles floating on the surface and smiled "Da always told us that meant money coming our way. There's a lot here so maybe I'll find some today."

Lizzie looked past Maggie to the sun shine and blue skies over the Gulf. A breeze was moving through the palm fronds causing them to wave gently. Wanting to enjoy this time with her mother she said "Tell me about your Dad."

Maggie brightened when she spoke. "He was a fine man. Tall and slim and a hard worker. Everyone loved him. Honest and kind. An old dog showed up at the door one day. Momma said to send him away but when we all begged to keep him; it was Da who said yes. I remember her saying we can't afford to feed another soul but he just shook his head and patted the dog saying he wasn't a big one and wouldn't eat much. He was a fine man," Maggie said again then fell into silence looking out the window.

Chapter 17

On Saturday, at the end of June, Lizzie and Dan were up by 6:00. He had to be out of the house early for an 8:00 AM tee time. Pepper rubbed against Lizzie's legs as she poured coffee in matching mugs.

"I did feed you Pepper. I promise to play with you when Dan is gone," Lizzie said picking up the tray and heading off to the bedroom.

Lizzie drank her coffee sitting on the edge of the bed as Dan got ready. He had his coffee and a bagel on the dresser, talking about the day and eating as he pulled the white golf shirt from the walk-in closet he sort of shared with his wife.

"Lizzie you have too many clothes. They are starting to take over my side of the closet"

"No more, I promise I'll do some sorting and get rid of a few things."

Dan laughed. "Sure you will." Long ago they learned to pick their battles. Space in the closet didn't warrant anything but a comment and a smile on both sides. Lizzie put 'clean the closet' on her mental To Do list for the summer.

At the door Dan took Lizzie in his arms and kissed her softly. "Enjoy your day Lizzie. Have fun. No matter what happens, stay in the moment with her."

"Easy for you to say. You are heading out for the day. I'll have her here to myself." She sighed and kissed him lightly on the lips. "I know what you are saying. I will try."

* * *

Sitting at the breakfast bar Lizzie finished her coffee and read the St Pete Times, enjoying a few minutes of quiet. She heard a noise coming from down the hall. Thinking Maggie was awake and maybe confused she got up to check on her. As she opened the door Lizzie heard Maggie moaning softly and thrashing about in the bed.

"Mom, wake up," Lizzie said walking to the bed and reaching out to touch her mother

"No, no," cried Maggie as she slapped at Lizzie's hand.

"Mom, wake up," Lizzie repeated. "You're having a bad dream."

Maggie's eyes opened quickly. "What are you doing in my house?" she demanded.

"You were having a bad dream. Everything is okay," said Lizzie. "You're at my house. You spent the night. Dan has gone to play golf and you are I are spending the day together."

"Danny? Where is Danny?" she asked as she scrunched the sheet up to her neck.

"Golfing. He'll be home later."

"Good. I'll talk to Danny." Maggie said as she released her tight hold on the sheets. "I need to get up now."

"Let me help," said Lizzie as she took Maggie's arm. "You get ready and I'll make you a cup of tea."

Maggie looked at Lizzie and smiled shyly. She sat in the bed, still holding the sheet tightly and looking around the room as if seeing it for the first time. "Ah, I'd love a cup of tea dear. I'll get ready. Do I have any clothes here?"

"Yes Mom. They're hanging in the closet. Your underwear is in that top drawer," Lizzie said pointing to the tall dresser. "Do you want me to stay and help you?"

"Yes dear. That would be nice," Maggie said letting go of the sheet and sitting on the edge of the bed. Her hair was messy and with no makeup on she looked older and delicate.

Lizzie felt her heart lurch in pain watching the confusion on her mother's face. She had been so strong and independent, well except for her reliance on Daddy, Lizzie thought as she took her mother's arm and gently helped her to her feet. "The bathroom is right over there. I'll get you a pair of white slacks and a nice top. Do you want to take a shower now?"

"Could I?" Maggie asked like a child wanting a special treat.

"Of course. Do you want to do that now?"

"Yes dear," Maggie said in a soft voice.

"I'll start the shower and leave your clothes here on the bed."

"That would be lovely dear. Then could I have a cup of tea? I don't want to be a bother but I would love a cup of tea."

"Sure Mom. It's no bother. I'll bring you some tea to drink while you get dressed then I'll fix you breakfast. We can eat on the deck if you like. It's not too warm yet."

Maggie emerged half an hour later looking more like herself. She had combed her hair and put on some makeup and the ever present lipstick. No matter what was going on Maggie wore lipstick. She always said she felt naked without it.

The women relaxed, sitting on the deck, looking at the blue water and feeling the warm breeze. The remnants of breakfast lay about the table as Lizzie sipped the last of her coffee. "What would you like to do today?" she asked turning to Maggie who did not respond. She was intent on watching the large brown pelicans flying nearby. One dove into the water and came soaring up with a wriggling fish in its beak.

"Oh look. Did you see that?" cried Maggie clapping her hand to her chest. "I don't ever remember seeing birds that big."

"Yes, they're fun to watch," said Lizzie smiling. "It never gets old. Sometimes we see the dolphins swimming out there in the water."

"Do you catch them?" asked Maggie. "Are they good to

eat?"

"No, no Mom. You don't catch dolphin. You watch them swim. You don't eat them," said Lizzie with a look of disgust on her face.

"Well I didn't know," said Maggie looking down at her hands.

"I have to go to the grocery store. Let's get ready now and go before it gets too late," said Lizzie.

"You know, I never hear from anyone," said Maggie still looking down at her hands. "They never write to me. Why?"

"I don't know," said Lizzie. "Do you write to them?"

"No... not for a while. I did tell them where I was going but I never heard from anyone. You never wrote to me either," Maggie said looking intently at Lizzie.

"I did write when I was away at school," Lizzie protested. "Maybe not every week but I wrote."

"Maybe I should write to Bridget. Maybe it would be okay now."

"Sure Mom. You can do that when we get back from the store."

By the time they returned from running errands Maggie had forgotten about writing letters. She was content to sit in the family room and look out the window at the water and the large brown pelicans flying by.

* * *

Sunday was a good day. Early Mass, lunch on the beach at Woody's and a quiet afternoon of reading the paper. Dan was grilling chicken for dinner and would make an everything salad with his special dressing. The salad consisted of every leftover in the refrigerator, a few cans of whatever was in the cupboard and his world famous, or so he thought, dressing. It was always surprisingly good.

The two women sat on the deck as Dan took over the kitchen, singing loudly to the old Bob Dylan song, *Forever Young*. Maggie, not remembering she had been invited to stay the summer, leaned over to whisper to Lizzie "Would you mind if I stayed a few more days?"

"Stay as long as you like, Mom. We can go over to the condo after I get off work tomorrow to pick up more clothes and whatever else you need."

"Are you sure Danny won't mind?"

"You know you are always welcome. He loves you," Lizzie said smiling.

"I know. I know," she said, her words barely audible.

After dinner they made plans for the coming week. Picking up clothes, dinner out and dinner at home. Dan would be working late but Lizzie would be home early. Maggie was always calmer when Dan was around, especially in the evenings when she was apt to be more confused. She would keep her eyes on him as they sat in the family room watching TV. A slight smile on her face. They didn't know if she understood the show they were watching but if they laughed, Maggie laughed. If they were quiet and intent on the show she would be as well. When it was over she would often thank them for allowing her to be with them. Those were the nights they both knew she had no idea who they were. Just two nice people who spent time with her.

Chapter 18

The holiday arrived with a bright sun and a humid breeze. Rain was called for later in the day. Lizzie kept an eye on the sky watching out her kitchen window as large billowing grey clouds formed out in the gulf.

"No rain, no rain," she kept repeating between each sip of coffee. It was not yet 8:00 AM and she was on her third cup. She and Dan had eaten breakfast earlier and now she was getting ready to make her favorite seven layer salad. Her kids loved it as did most of the Gee-kids. Gee-kids? When had they started referring to the grandkids as Gee-kids? She would have to ask someone. Before she could finish her thought the phone was ringing. "Aunt Lizzie I'm bringing an extra plate of brownies just for Uncle Dan. I want to be able to bring them in and hide them right away so no one else gets them but him. He is my favorite uncle and I want to do a little something special."

"Don't say that. What would Uncle Ian think if he heard that?"

"He won't hear it if you don't tell him. Where can I put the brownies?"

"Darling, just put them in our bedroom on the dresser," Lizzie laughed as she spoke. "They may be just for Uncle Dan but rest assured, I plan on eating one or two so maybe you had better add a few more to the plate. And, I promise I won't say a word."

Maggie was standing in the doorway to the kitchen. She looked rested and seemed eager for a party. Her hair was combed and her make-up perfect. She was wearing white capris with a red, white and blue striped boat neck shirt. Strappy blue sandals on her feet. "What was that all about?" she asked Lizzie her voice thin as she played with the cross at her neck.

"Nothing, nothing at all," replied Lizzie.

Maggie twisted her hands and looked concerned but let it go. "Mind if I fix a cup of tea?" she asked.

"Mom, you don't have to ask. Help yourself anytime. Or better yet, let me make you a cup now."

"No, no. I'll get it. I don't want to be a bother," she said. Almost in a whisper she asked, "What's the big secret?"

Lizzie laughed as she saw the concerned look on her mom's face. "No big secret. It's nothing at all. I promise."

Maggie stood by the stove, looking confused so Lizzie moved over and took her by the arm. "Here, sit. Let me do this for you."

"Well Grand Maggie," Lizzie said as she put the tea kettle on to boil, "everyone should be here by noon. We'll eat at 2:00 or 3:00." Grand Maggie. What a name. They all had been together when Ian and Rose brought their first child home. Sam picked up the baby and held him close to his chest. Everyone had quietly watched the proud grandpa hold his first grandchild. "You're a lucky little boy, Thomas. You have me for a grandpa but you have Maggie for a grandma. She's not just any old grandma she's a Grand Maggie. The finest, funniest, most magical woman in the world. A Grand Maggie she is. We are all lucky to have her in our lives," Sam spoke almost in a whisper.

Maggie's checks reddened and she waved her hand, "Oh Sam."

The name stuck. Whenever anyone mentioned Maggie to Thomas or any grandchild as they came along it was always 'Grand Maggie.' She even signed her cards and letters to the grandkids that way.

She had a way with the little ones. When no one else

could stop the crying or whining Maggie would step in and gather the overwhelmed youngster in her arms. She would whisper some secret words that charmed and were not to be shared. The tears stopped and after a few kisses and a bit more whispering the child would run off in a fit of giggles.

Lizzie had asked her oldest daughter Gabby, when she was five, what Grand Maggie had told to make her feel better.

"It's a secret Mommy..." she whispered, looking around, then added, "If you promise not to tell..."

"I promise," Lizzie stated solemnly raising her right hand to her heart.

"Grand Maggie knows the fairies living nearby," she said leaning close. "They hurt when we cry. Hurt like being pricked with a pin." Her eyes scrunched up in pretend pain, then continued with an impish grin, "But, when we smile or laugh they feel full of happiness like we are when we eat ice cream cones. The fairies watch out for us Mommy. So, Grand Maggie said we need to watch out for them and not hurt them. No more tears," she declared raising her hands, palms up.

Everyone brought their favorite side dish or desert to share. The kitchen counter was covered by bowls and platters. Even though there was a second refrigerator in the garage there wasn't enough room. "We had better get this food organized and the mob fed or we're in trouble," Lizzie called out to her four daughters. The before dinner munchies were being set up on a long blue and white covered table on the deck.

"We'll get some food for the little ones to tide them over and then take a breather. Mom, we have plenty of time and we all want you to relax. So take it easy. We're not eating dinner for a couple of hours. Here are a couple of beers. Go give Dad a hug," said Gabby, the more take charge of her children.

Dan ruled over the grill. He was checking to make sure he had enough gas and all his utensils were clean and ready to go. Lizzie walked up behind him, encircled his chest with her arms and laid her head against his back.

"A beer for me? You're the perfect wife, Lizzie," he said putting down the spatula, taking the beer and putting his arms over hers.

Maggie watched Dan closely from a lounge chair nearby and softly whispered to Lizzie as she sat down beside her, "I know him from somewhere, but I'm not sure where. He lived down the lane across from the McGuire's, the ones with the big horse. Remember them? There is something about him ... something about him and Bridget ..."

Lizzie wanted to tell her she didn't know those people. She couldn't know them because she had never been to Ireland. But Maggie was enjoying herself and Lizzie knew she could ask another time. The memories might come back. Besides, there were too many people around to have any kind of meaningful conversation. The Gee-kids had not seen much of Grand Maggie lately so as they arrived they headed straight for her chair for hugs and kisses.

The party was a success. Ian and Rose reveled in the fact that all five of their children showed up. It was not often the schedules allowed such a gathering. "Lizzie, they did this for Grand Maggie," Ian said as he watched Charles, his middle son and wife Bobbie line a few of the Gee- kids up at the edge of the pool for a
race. "They're all here, except for Melinda and Chuck."

"Oh, they'll be here," Lizzie stated. "I just got a call. They changed their plans so we could all be together. George brought his camera and will set up a photo shoot later this afternoon. We don't want to miss an opportunity like this though I'm not sure his lens is big enough to get us all in the same picture."

Throughout the day Maggie spoke of Sam. When she knew she was speaking to someone in the family she referred to Sam as your Dad or Grandpa Sam. But most of the day she was laughing and regaling the group with stories of her Sam as if she had just met them all for the first time.

"My Sam, My Sam. What a handsome fella. We were at the hall in town. I don't remember where exactly but there was a band and everyone was all dressed up. The soldiers and sailors in uniform and us gals in the best clothes we could find. Why, I even had a pair of nylons that night. I'm not sure where I got those but I do remember wearing them. Nylons and my black dancing shoes."

Maggie stretched out her legs and looked at her feet. She seemed surprised to see pink toenail polish and blue sandals. "What happened next?" asked Lizzie's granddaughter Hannah.

With a joyous smile Maggie continued. "There was a stage with a band. Not a big band but enough to make the most beautiful music and get us all out on the floor dancing. Most of the girls were with someone and I was with a soldier I had been seeing. Handsome redheaded soldier from the states, Midwest I think. Can't remember his name. We were dancing, slow dancing and laughing about something silly. My Sam walked on to the dance floor, tapped the boy on the shoulder saying in his deep commanding voice, 'Excuse me. That's my girl you have in your arms.' Well this soldier was slighter in build and shorter than my Sam. I remember the color rose in his cheeks all the way to his hairline. He sputtered and said 'Yes, Sir. Sorry Sir,' and released me."

"Yes Sir," said little Nate as he saluted his great grandmother.

Maggie laughed as the child scampered over to her and climbed on her lap. After giving him a quick kiss on the cheek she continued, "Sam took me in his arms without missing a step and danced me right off the floor and over to a table. I tell you it was love at first sight. For both of us. We talked until the band stopped playing. We talked until the morning came. We laughed and talked and walked through the town. I don't know what we talked about but we knew we were meant to be together. Within a month we were engaged and married seven weeks later. He swept me off my feet and onto a boat headed for America."

Everyone loved to hear this story though it had been told a thousand times before. It didn't matter. It was their family love story. Sam and Maggie. They were meant to be together. Best friends, soul mates, lovers. Their story gave everyone hope that someday, they too, would find love, the magical kind that Sam and Maggie had. It's what Lizzie always wanted in a marriage and what she found with Dan.

Lizzie was the first to leave Ohio. She didn't plan on leaving forever; she wanted to leave the cold weather behind for at least a little while. She didn't count on meeting Dan, the man who changed her world the way Sam had changed Maggie's. She knew love at first sight was not only possible but according to Maggie, very probable. It happened to Maggie and Sam. It could happen to her. She met Dan at the library during the second month of school at Florida State University in Tallahassee. Getting settled, new classes and studying was keeping her busy but she needed to read a book, a regular book just for fun. She knocked into Dan standing in the checkout line in front of her. They both felt the connection that first time they looked into each other's eyes. Now, after over thirty years, the attraction and love was even stronger.

The entire clan was gathered on the deck with the dazzling sun playing off the brilliant blue of the Gulf waters. The black clouds had receded and with them the threat of rain. Sea gulls and pelicans soared through the sky. Dan offered a short prayer of thanksgiving for the great food, the beautiful day and the joy of having all of the family together. He finished by saying, "Sam may not be here in the flesh but he is here in each of the Gee-kids and Great Gee-kids and in all of our hearts." A few seconds of almost painful silence was broke when Sarah, the youngest grandchild of Kevin and Becca, let go with a loud wail.

"Do not pinch your sister Lilly," Melinda whispered.

"I'm hungry," came the defiant reply.

The tension was broken as Dan hollered out, "Let's eat."

Chapter 19

It was a loud, boisterous party with too much of everything which made it just about perfect. After the meal and before the deserts were laid out Ian got everyone on the deck for photos. George, Gabby's husband was an amateur photographer. He quickly got the three families organized with Maggie in the center and took a treasure trove of photos. First, each family with kids and grandkids posed. Then he took on the monumental task of obtaining a photo of them all, Maggie, her three children and their spouses, the eleven Gee-kids and the twenty-nine Great Gee-kids. Somehow he managed to take several pictures of the fifty-seven people all smiling, looking at the camera with their eyes open.

Dan picked up the last of the brownies from the red platter Maureen had brought. Dan could never get enough of those brownies. It was a good thing Lizzie refused to make them for him. When he had seen them on the counter he had almost snagged the tray and hid it in the laundry room for himself. That was when Maureen told him in a whispered voice that she had made a tray just for him. "Aunt Lizzie knows where they are so you may have to share with her."

"It was a good day," he said popping the last brownie in his mouth. "Maggie had fun even if she didn't know who everyone was most of the time."

"Do you think they knew that?" asked Lizzie. "Do they know our mom is gone? Their Grand Maggie is gone?"

Dan put his right arm around her shoulder and hefted the white trash bag over his left. "My dear, let's take a walk." Lizzie snuggled, giggled and walked to the alley with Dan. He released his hold on her to lift the dumpster lid and toss in the bag.

"Lizzie the only thing that matters is Maggie had a good day. It doesn't matter if she knows us. It matters that we know her." He cradled her face in his hands and kissed her lightly on the lips then wrapped her in his arms for a long sensuous kiss.

"We have to get back for the fireworks and Maggie," Lizzie reminded him.

"Sure, but later we'll be having our own fireworks," he said with a laugh as he patted her butt.

* * *

The three of them sat in the lounge chairs, on the top level of the deck. Lizzie in the middle, holding Dan's hand with her left and a mug of decaf coffee in her right. The fireworks were scheduled to start just after nine. The first burst of light and sound brought a slight gasp from Maggie.

"We had fireworks in London," she stated. "Very loud fireworks. I don't remember them being as pretty as these. It was the first night I saw my Sam."

Lizzie turned to Dan. She whispered, "They didn't have fireworks in London during the war. Those were bombs. And Daddy... "

Dan shook his head and squeezed her hand. She said nothing more.

Maggie squinted as if looking back in time. "I was so scared that night. I was trying to get away from all the noise. I ran and ran. The smoke and ash and noise. Crying. Not just babies crying, grown men crying. The harsh stench of smoke from burning wood and cars and...." She stopped abruptly reaching for the cross at her neck. After a spectacular burst of color in the sky she said, "I was sitting on the floor. It was cold and dirty. My back was against the icy tile wall. I could feel it, the terrible bone chilling cold they used to call it, though my coat."

Maggie wrapped her arms around herself as if trying to ward off the remembered cold. "I didn't have my gloves and my hat must have blown off somewhere. I was so afraid of what was happening. I was alone and had no one. They were all gone. It was just a pile of rubble. I had seen the door with the lace curtain blowing through the window but the door led to nowhere. It was as if it had been built to open on to a pile of bricks, not a room at all."

She closed her eyes and let out a low moan. "I had run and run and ended up there on that ugly floor. Then I looked up and saw my Sam. Well, he wasn't my Sam then. He squatted down in front of me and said 'There, there, honey. There, there.' Just like you would say to a frightened child. I was crying and he pulled a crisp white handkerchief out of a pocket and wiped my checks. 'Just a few tears and a little bit of dirt,' he said."

Lizzie and Dan did not look at the glorious bursts of red, blue, white and gold in the sky but at Maggie, so small and frail in the large wooden chair.

"I don't know how he knew I was lost. I don't know how he knew to find me. Then he was sitting on the floor with his arm around my shoulders holding me to his chest. I could feel his scratchy uniform and cold metal buttons on my face ... and he smelled of smoke and wet wool. But I was safe. I was safe for the first time in so long. No one was going to get me. No one would hurt me. I wanted to stay right there with his arms around me and hear him say 'There, there, honey. There, there.'"

Just then there was the crashing boom of the fireworks grand finale.

"Jesus, Mary and Joseph. That scared the life out of me," yelped Maggie as she was pulled from the past and dropped in the present.

That was not the story of Maggie and Sam that was told

earlier in the day or any day before. Now Lizzie was hearing about smoke, cold tile and crying people. She had seen fear on Maggie's face when she was talking but now she was calm, here in the moment watching the fireworks grand finale. The fireworks were over and so was Maggie's venture into the past.

Lizzie had to ask, "How did you and Daddy meet?"

"Oh darling, you've heard that story a hundred times. We met dancing at a party."

The moment was gone. Lizzie didn't know if or when it would be back.

Chapter 20

Dan, Lizzie and Maggie got up early for Sunday Mass. Lizzie delivered a pot of tea and buttered toast on a tray to Maggie in her room.

"I'll be ready soon darling," Maggie told her as he stood in the bedroom in her nightgown. "I'm going to take a quick shower. Thank you for the tea. What a lovely thing to do. I so enjoy a cup of tea. Don't you dear?"

"Yes, I do. Do you need any help here?" Lizzie asked knowing her mom did not recognize her. Maybe later in the day she would.

"No dear, I'm just fine."

Dan and Lizzie had their coffee and bagels at the breakfast bar and scanned the paper as they waited. "Mom seems fine today. I was worried the party would wear her out completely but she seems energized." Lizzie sighed, "But, she doesn't know who I am. I don't even know who she thinks I am. Just some woman being nice to her? But Dan, what she said last night. She was talking about the bombing of London. That she met Daddy during the bombing of London, not some USO party."

"We don't know that Lizzie. She may be remembering a movie or a book," Dan said, glancing at the sports page.

"Really? That's what you think? You saw her face. She was scared as if reliving a terrible event," Lizzie said leaning forward to rest her arms on the counter.

Looking up he said, "I know. Maybe it is how they met and they didn't want to share that story. The one they made up is prettier. An easy one to tell you kids. Why tell your kids about a horrible time in your life? We don't share the rough time with our kids. I don't think if that were our story I would share with the girls. Would you?" Dan asked, challenging Lizzie.

"No, maybe not. I understand when we were young. But why not tell us later?" Lizzie asked getting up for more coffee.

"When? When is a good time to tell your kids you have lied to them all these years? Everyone loves the Maggie and Sam story. It is legend in this family. You going to tell your brothers?" asked Dan holding out his cup for more coffee.

"I don't know," Lizzie shrugged. "They should know, but how do I tell them? We don't even know if it is true."

"Exactly my point. If Maggie tells them and they talk to you fine. But what good does it do to tell some awful war story? Especially, as you say, we don't even know if it is true," Dan said reaching to take her hand. "Look, just let it go. It doesn't help to dwell on any negative stuff now. Every day is different. Let's just enjoy the good moments."

"Easy for you to say. She's not your mom. Your mom knows who you are. You can talk to her about anything. I can't talk to my mother about the past, the present or the future. The best I can do is make her a cup of tea," Lizzie said gripping the mug tightly in her hand and glaring at Dan.

"Lizzie. What do you want me to say? This is just what we are dealing with now." Dan leaned over to give her a kiss on the cheek.

"I know I am whining but Dan this is so difficult," Lizzie said as her eyes filled with tears.

Pepper came to the stool Lizzie was sitting on and reached up to touch her leg. Absently Lizzie reached down to pet the cat behind the ears. She could hear the contented purr and said softly "You're a good girl, Pepper."

They sat this way for a few more minutes in silence then Maggie emerged with a smile and declared "I'm ready. Let's go you two. We don't want to be late."

Pepper sauntered over to Maggie and rubbed against her leg. Reaching down she repeated the actions of her daughter and the cat purred loudly.

They rode the three miles to the church without talking. Maggie, sitting in the back, was calm and peaceful. Dan reached over the console to Lizzie in the passenger seat and squeezed her hand. Lizzie only looked out the window lost in her own unsettled thoughts.

"Well ladies, what do you want to do today? A ride in the boat? Lunch at Woody's beach bar? Reading by the pool? Want to be lazy or do something?"

"I'm up for whatever you want," said Lizzie without any enthusiasm. She really wanted to sit by herself, curled up in a chair, reading. She wanted to forget what was going on in her life, just for a few hours.

Dan knew Lizzie needed a break. "We haven't had any time alone since you came to visit Maggie. What do you say to a lunch date with me? Lizzie has a new book she is dying to read so we can leave her to her book and leftovers."

"Ah, I would love it Danny," came Maggie's quick response.

Chapter 21

Lizzie was stretched out on the beige suede sofa in the family room. A puffy pillow was at her back against the armrest. Pepper was asleep at her feet. She could see some of the greenery in the back yard but not the water. She had not bothered with lunch. Instead she had a bowl of grapes and a glass of ice tea on the coffee table. As promised, she was reading her new novel by Michael Connelley when Dan and Maggie arrived home.

Maggie kissed her quickly on the top of the head. "I'm going to take a bit of a nap, dear," she said as she slowly looked around to see where she was supposed to go before walking down the hall to the guest room.

Dan bent down and kissed his wife. "Lizzie, how 'bout we grab a couple of beers and sit out by the pool? I need to talk to you about Maggie." Before she could protest, he took the book from her hands, marked the page and offered his hand to help her from the sofa.

Danny recounted the story Maggie told at lunch. No mention of a fire, no mention of the family dying, only that she had not heard from them since she moved here to London. "Lizzie, by the time she went to London her family was dead. She talked as if they might even come visit. What happened to your mom back then?"

Lizzie only knew the merest details of the stories her parents had told, the house fire, the USO dance, the move to America. Maggie and Sam looked forward, never backward. "'The past is over and done. Nothing you can do to change it. It is the future you own, the future you rule, the future you make for yourself.' That's what Daddy always said. I don't have a clue about any of this. Do you suppose it's the disease? She's confused. Maybe you're right. She's blending her life with movies or books," said Lizzie, not believing this at all. She felt her mom was reliving her life, her real life in the stories she had begun to share.

"Lizzie, we were seated in a booth. The fans whirred overhead. The juke box was playing *Wouldn't It Be Nice* by the Beach Boys. The stools at the bar were filled with a few tourist, but mostly regulars. I asked if she wanted a nice cold beer and she said, 'Not a beer, Danny, but I will take a whiskey and water, neat please.' When's the last time she asked for a whiskey? Then, out of the blue she asked me, 'Danny, did you marry her?'" Leaning forward Dan smiled and said "I know how she feels about people living together without the sacrament of marriage, so I said sure I married Lizzie and I'm a lucky man for having her. Then Maggie cocks her head, raises her eyebrows and said 'Lizzie? We never called her Lizzie. Always Bridget. Oh, maybe if she was in trouble, Da would say Bridget Elizabeth. Never Lizzie. Where ever did you get that?'"

He ran his hands through his hair and continued. "I didn't know what to say but she didn't notice, she just kept talking. She said 'Bridget was mad for you Danny. You were mad for each other.' Then she asked me again. 'You never married her?' When I asked, who's Bridget? she laughed 'Oh, Danny, my sister Bridget Elizabeth Malone. Did something happen between you?'"

Dan was so excited in the telling of his story Lizzie didn't want to interrupt. She sat back, watching him closely and look a long pull of the beer.

"Sandy was our waitress today. You know how chatty she can be. So, when she showed up, I just ordered ice tea for me and hot tea for Maggie. She had already forgotten about the whiskey. I said we needed a few minutes. I wanted to keep

Maggie talking. We know so little about her from back then, I wanted to hear what she had to say. I wish you'd been there," Dan said patting Lizzie's knee.

"Me too," Lizzie leaned forward in her chair.

"She asked me again, 'did something happen?' So I asked her, "What do you think happened Maggie?"

"I swear Lizzie, she even had a brogue when she said 'Now why would I know? We all thought you'd get married and have a houseful of little ones. Bridget so loved babies.' Then she shook her head from side to side and laughed. She even blushed. 'Oh Danny we had no idea how you got those babies just knew we wanted them.'"

Lizzie looked at the bottle of beer in her hand and realized she had pealed the label off. "Dan this is amazing. I wish I had been there, but... maybe she wouldn't have talked to you like she did."

"I know. I thought of that too. She talked as if I knew the people she grew up with or lived in her neighborhood. She asked if I remembered Mr. and Mrs. Casey down the road. She said they had a dozen or more kids and her Momma would say she didn't know how they found the time to have all those babies. 'Oh Danny' she smiled at me and said 'We didn't understand then but I sure do now.'"

"She said, 'that woman always had a baby on her hip and a smile for everyone. Life was hard then Danny but Mrs. Casey seemed to know how to find the joy in it. I have thought of her often over the years. God Bless her soul, I wonder what ever became of her and her family?' She actually said that Lizzie." Dan said leaning back in his chair and wiping his hand on his thigh.

"I didn't want to talk about babies with your mom any more so I asked her to tell me more about Bridget."

"She talked like I knew her. 'Wasn't she a pretty thing Danny? All that red hair and huge green eyes. She had the boys looking at her but all Bridget ever saw was you.' Me. Like

I was this guy she knew."

"Then she told me about Liam," Dan said excitedly. "Have you ever heard her talk about a Liam?"

"Never. Dan this whole thing is so weird," Lizzie said shaking her head.

Dan took another pull from the bottle. "Well listen to this. She tells me she was sweet on Liam. She thinks his last name is Taylor. She and Bridget would walk home from school making plans. Plans to go to America. She said Liam's daddy owned a small store in town on Market Street across from his Uncle's pub. She asked me the name of it, then she laughed and said it was 'The Rearing Horse or The Roaring something.' Can you believe it?" Dan asked his eyes wide and a huge grin on his face. "Anyway, he worked in the grocery store and she would flirt with him but was too nervous to do more than smile. She even told me he would sneak her candy when his daddy wasn't looking. Candy. Can you believe it?"

Dan started to laugh and sit forward in his chair. "She said she didn't want to eat it because his hand had touched it but she had her sweet tooth even back then so no matter how much she wanted to keep it, she ate it. Lizzie, watching her was amazing. Maggie smiled and laughed like old times. The lines on her face had softened; the feisty twinkle was back in her eyes. I loved seeing her like that."

"Oh Dan, I wish I was there, to see her like she was," Lizzie moaned.

"Then she said 'When you talked of moving to America,' like I was this Danny guy, 'even though the war was on, Bridget and I connived ways to have Liam join you. You know, so the four of us could go off to live the golden dream of life in America. How silly we were back then. We had no idea of real life.'"

"Just then Sandy's back at the table saying 'What'll you have?' Maggie seemed confused as she looked around the restaurant, at the water out the window and the tables filled with laughing folks eating their fish sandwiches and curly fries. She said 'I'm not that hungry, Dan.' Now she called me Dan. So, I ordered her a basket of grouper nuggets and fries. She just nodded and raised her right hand to her pat at her hair, you know how she does."

"After Sandy left I asked her is Bridget your only sister."

"Lizzie she said "Of course not. There were eight of us, six girls and two boys. Mama lost a couple along the way. Miscarriages, though we didn't know much about it. There was Bridget the oldest, then me, then Molly, Kathleen, Bernadette, Maureen and the two boys, the twins, little Kevin and Ian."

"Kevin and Ian?" asked Lizzie. "Mom said there were only three other kids, all younger than she, all girls Kathleen, Bernadette and Maureen."

"Yeah. I didn't know what to say when she asked me 'How are they? I never hear from any of them since I moved here to London.' She kept shaking her head and saying repeatedly I never hear from any of them."

Lizzie was puzzled and didn't know how to respond. As far as all of them knew Maggie's family was dead. Both her parents and her three younger sisters died in a house fire in 1943, before she went to London. The fire was the reason she left Ireland. She had stayed with neighbors for a few months but in those times it was too much to take on one more mouth to feed. She had no close family in Kilcoty. Aunt Agatha, a spinster aunt, as Maggie always referred to her, took her in. She worked in a shoe factory until she met Sam and moved to America.

"Just before the food came Maggie seemed sort of back to normal, at least back to here and now. But then, she looked down at her hands then back to me with the saddest look in her eyes and asked 'Danny what has happened to me?'"

"Before I could answer Sandy arrived. The distraction brought her back more to the present and she smiled that gracious smile of hers as the plate of grouper nuggets were put down in front of her." Dan said with a shake of his head. "All I kept thinking was I wished you were here. She got quiet after that and we ate in silence. I didn't know what to make of it all. When we were done eating she told me she was feeling a bit off and wanted to go home to lie down. Lizzie, she knows something is wrong but doesn't remember the conversations we have had with her about the Alzheimer's. She is trying to get control of her thoughts but...you can see she is failing."

Chapter 22

Feeling guilty about leaving Samantha with all the clients and paperwork Lizzie called her at home. "I've taken off so much time off work already but I just don't know what to do. Mom is so confused and then not confused. She knows where she is and then we could be in Ohio or England or Ireland. I'll get some help, but for now, if you don't mind I'm going to take a few more days off."

"Honey, we are fine here. Everything is under control. Take whatever time you need. You covered for me in the past when my kids were in the hospital. Don't you worry about a thing here at the office. Just take care of Maggie and yourself. If I need you I will call."

Relieved, Lizzie put down the phone and walked into the living room. Her mother was sitting on the brown suede side chair with a picture of Sam in her lap. Pepper was sprawled out on the floor at her feet. The photo, one of Lizzie's favorites, was taken right after she and Dan bought their boat, called the Lizzie Lou, her childhood nickname. Sam is standing at the helm with a captain's hat on, wearing a white golf shirt and crisp khaki shorts. His tanned face showed some wrinkles but mostly laughs lines as he grinned widely for the camera and saluted. This is how she remembers him. Smiling and happy, facing every day with joyous expectations.

"I miss him," said Maggie tracing his jaw with her finger.

"Me too, Mom."

"How long has it been?"

"Just since April."

"How long?" Maggie asked again with a puzzled look

on her face.

"Three months...just three months," Lizzie said her voice faltering and tears welling in her eyes. She turned away.

"Are you sure? What about the others?" Maggie asked still gazing at the photo of Sam in her lap.

"What others?"

"What became of Bridget? Is she dead too? Are they all gone?" Maggie asked looking up raising her hand to hold the cross at her neck.

"Who are they?" Lizzie asked as she moves closer and sits on the matching beige love seat.

"It doesn't matter anymore. My Sam is gone. I want to go home," Maggie said sinking deeper in the chair.

"Oh no. It's not a good idea for you to go home alone now. You promised Dan you would stay through the summer. We both want you here."

"Where is Danny? Can he tell me about Bridget? I know I saw her not that long ago. She was helping me. Where did she go? Is she dead too?"

"I don't know what to say. I don't know who Bridget is."

"Of course you do. Bridget is my sister. She was at my condo. Maybe you weren't there. Where's Danny? He can help."

"He's over to Gabby and George's. They had a problem with a toilet and he's going to help fix it," Lizzie said with a deep sigh.

"He's such a good boy. He helped me. Do you remember? I can't remember it all, but he helped me."

"Dan may be late tonight so I'll fix us something light for dinner. He'll eat with the kids."

Maggie's grip tightened on the silver frame as she continued to stare at the photo, lost in her own memories. "I think I should write a letter to Bridget," Maggie stated in a firm voice.

"Mom I don't know who Bridget is. I don't know how

to reach her," Lizzie said as she stood up and started for the kitchen her shoulders slumped.

"Oh, all we have to do is address it to Bridget Malone, Kells, Ireland. It will get to her. Everyone knows the Malones in Kells."

"Kells? But I thought you were from Kilcoty?"

"Kilcoty? Darling, who told you that? I was born in Kells, County Meath and went to school there. We all did. I didn't leave until the after the war started. I really must get in touch with Bridget," Maggie said.

Lizzie's closed her eyes as she leaned against the breakfast bar. "We'll do that tomorrow."

"I can do it now while you are getting dinner ready or do you need me to help? I don't want you to feel like I'm a bother. I can set the table or fix the salad?"

"No. You just sit there. I'll have it ready in a few minutes."

"Whatever you say darling. I'll just sit here and visit with my Sam," Maggie said in a quiet voice as she ran a finger over Sam's face in the photo. "My Sam."

* * *

Over dinner of a garden salad with grilled chicken and fresh crusty bread, hot tea for Maggie and glass of wine for herself, Lizzie tried to get her mom to talk about Ireland. "What kind of house did you live in growing up Mom?"

"It wasn't big, not like this house. Just three tiny bedrooms, a kitchen and living room all together. Oh, we had a massive fireplace. Momma would sit near it in the winter sewing. You know she made all our clothes. She had a machine but so much was done by hand. The hems, the buttons and of course fixing the clothes my brothers wore. They were such boys," Maggie said with a shake of her head and a wide smile. "Always into everything, tearing out the knees of the pants or growing out of them. Mama had a needle in her hand most evenings. No electric lights, just the oil lamps. I can see her so clearly. She was a beauty. Long auburn hair and green eyes, like you. My Da would always say 'Ah Mary, you are such a beauty. What are you doing with the likes of me?'"

Lizzie had stopped eating and sat staring at her mom. Maggie had never really talked about her family. Whenever asked she would say it was too sad to talk about and change the subject. Lizzie watched her sip her tea and wanted to ask questions but feared saying anything would break the spell.

Maggie looked at the forkful of salad, staring at it as if she didn't know how it got into her hand, and then turned to Lizzie. "Where are they now? What happened to them?"

"I don't know Mom," Lizzie said no longer hungry.

"Ah, they were good people just trying to do the best they could. I wanted to go home. I thought they wanted to see me but I never heard from them. One letter, then nothing."

"Why didn't you go back after the war?"

"It wasn't safe. Since I didn't hear from Momma or Da or even Bridget, I knew it wasn't safe for me to return. Then there was Sam. He wanted to carry me off to America and I let him. Oh I loved him, still do," Maggie said looking around as if he were elsewhere in the room. "But... I wonder what happened to them. Why they didn't they ever write to me?"

"Did you try to contact them?" Lizzie asked.

Maggie looked up, fingering the cross at her neck. "No, I never did. I was afraid and now they may all be gone."

"Why did you leave Ireland?" Lizzie asked seeing the sadness etched across her mother's face but unable to stop probing.

"It was the incident. I had to leave or I don't know what would have become of me."

"What incident?" Lizzie asked reaching for her wine glass and taking a sip.

"It was so long ago. Does it matter anymore?" Maggie asked her hand holding tightly to the arm of her chair.

"I thought you might like to talk about it, talk about your family. I'd love to know more about them," Lizzie said as casually as she could while looking down at her plate of salad.

Maggie spoke as if she had not heard Lizzie's last statement. "Brendan was his name. It's my fault he's dead."

"Dead?" Lizzie said as her head snapped up and she looked at Maggie. "How could it be your fault?"

"I don't remember it all now. It was Brendan that lay dead and Liam was there. Danny and Bridget too." Maggie's eyes were wide now and the hand holding the fork was shaking slightly.

"What happened?" Lizzie asked, her mouth suddenly going dry, panic rising inside her.

"There was a lot of blood. On him and me. It was my fault," Maggie said in a whisper. "My fault. Liam said so." She looked around the room as if someone else was lurking nearby and could hear. "Who else is here?"

"No one Mom, just you and me," said Lizzie her own hand shaking as she picked up the wine glass and took a large swallow.

"I've never told anyone. I've never talked about it," said Maggie twisting in her chair to look out on the darkened deck. "Who's here?" she asked again.

"No one else is here just you and me. Please tell me about Liam," Lizzie said though she remembered Dan telling her Maggie spoke of a boy named Liam she had been sweet on so many years ago.

Turning back to the table with a smile on her face she said "Ah, you know Liam. He was the big one, well over six feet tall with broad shoulders and that messy thatch of dark red hair. Worked for his daddy at the store."

Lizzie wanted to know what happened to Brendan but Maggie seemed less agitated talking about Liam so she asked "Was he your boyfriend?"

"I was sweet on him for sure and he liked me too." Maggie smiled and her cheeks reddened. "I let him kiss me you know. Bridget had Danny. I so wanted a fella and Liam was grand."

"What happened ?"

Her smile was gone and it was like a dark cloud passed over Maggie's face. "It was the last time I saw him. That awful night. The last time I saw all of them. All of them except Danny. He helped me."

"Helped you how?" Lizzie asked not sure she wanted the answer.

"I got away from there. I thought I would go back but I never did," Maggie said looking around the room again.

"Why not?"

Maggie leaned across the table, her hand stretching to touch Lizzie's hand and said in a whisper, "He was dead. It was my fault."

"Mom this doesn't make any sense," Lizzie said while horrible pictures of a bloody dead man played across her mind. Speaking softly she added," You could never hurt anyone."

"You don't know what I have done," Maggie said with fierceness in her voice as she put down the fork and slowly picked up her cup of tea. "You only think you know me. I have my secrets."

"Of course I know you. You're my mother."

"What are you talking about? I don't have any children. I never married Liam. Not after what happened to Brendan," Maggie snapped.

Lizzie had heard Maggie deny she was her daughter before but every time it brought a fresh wave of sorrow. How could she not know I'm her daughter Lizzie thought? She remembers all this stuff from so many years ago and not me. Looking out past the pool, to the blue waters and the sun low in the clear sky, Lizzie only nodded her head and picked up her glass of wine. With her other hand she wiped away the few tears that fell on to her cheeks. "Okay," was the only word she could say.

Maggie, unaware of the hurt she had caused asked, "When is Danny going to be home?"

"Not till later. He's at Gabby's helping her and George with a toilet problem."

"He's a good worker that one. A good man," Maggie said with a smile.

"Yes he is," Lizzie said flatly.

Chapter 23

Lizzie hurried down the hall securing her hair in a silver clip at the nape of her neck. "Oh Pepper, just let me get through the day," she said to the cat trotting beside her like a small black shadow. Dressed in an ankle length, royal blue cotton skirt and white t-shirt she carried her silver hoop earrings in one hand and her favorite pair of silver sandals in the other. She wore them with everything, jeans, shorts, skirts. Her closets were filled with clothes but only a dozen pair of shoes. Not so many when compared with her mom who owned at least fifty pairs.

The two of them were going for pedicures today, a bit of relaxation at the Serenity Spa. It would be peaceful as long as Maggie didn't talk too much. Lizzie and Dan didn't know what to make of her stories. Truth? Fantasy? Outright lies? Melding of real and imagined? Sipping her coffee at the breakfast bar Lizzie glanced at the clock on the stove, 9:45. No need to check on Maggie just yet. The appointment wasn't until 11:00.

The bedroom door opened and Lizzie heard an odd sound. Slap, click. Slap, click. Maggie came down the hall wearing one shoe and clutching another to her chest. "My shoe broke," she said softly and held out the small heel in her right hand.

"Mom, I'm sorry. I know you love those sandals. We can get them fixed."

"We can?" Maggie asked as if Lizzie was going to wave a wand and the shoes would be magically repaired.

"Sure. There's a place in Seminole. After we get out

toes done we'll go over there," Lizzie said smiling.

"Our toes? What's wrong with my toes?" Maggie asked looking down at her feet.

"Nothing's wrong. We're getting a pedicure today. You'll need a different pair of shoes for now."

Maggie, standing lopsided, looked sadly at the two pieces in her hands. "Will they be fixed today?"

"Don't know, we'll see."

Maggie and Lizzie walked back to the bedroom. In her condo, the closets were orderly, slacks on wooden hangers, bright tops on plastic hangers and shoes displayed on special racks, sorted by style and color. Sam had the closets designed for Maggie's extensive wardrobe. But here, disarray was the rule. Pants and tops hung together, shoes strewn on the floor or mismatched on the shelf. Some clothes were piled on the floor at the foot of the bed, others tossed on the bed.

"What happened, Mom?" Lizzie asked looking around the room which had been straightened up yesterday.

"I don't know," Maggie said in a small voice.

"What do you mean you don't know? You are the only one here," Lizzie stated, emphasizing each word in a tone harsher than she had intended.

"Well, I didn't make the mess. I got dressed this morning and it was fine. Who else is here?" Maggie asked looking around the room and out into the hall.

"Just you and me," Lizzie said waving her hands about. "Just you and me."

"Maybe that other woman did it," said Maggie with one hand on her hip and the other pointing to the bathroom.

"Whatever." Lizzie sighed and bent over to pick up two silky shirts from the floor. "Pick out a pair of sandals and let's get going."

"We can't leave this mess," Maggie said standing with her arms at her sides, lips quivering. "What will that woman say if she sees this? She'll be angry and won't let me stay here."

"What woman?"

"You know. The one who lets me stay here. She's so nice," said Maggie her eyes shining with tears. "I don't want to upset her."

Lizzie felt her heart ache and quietly said "I'm that woman." Then turning to Maggie she said in a husky voice "We'll clean it all up later. Before that woman comes back."

"I don't have any shoes. That was my only pair." Maggie said with hands on her hips.

"No, these are all your shoes. Pick one. We're going to be late," Lizzie stated, mirroring Maggie with both hands on her hips.

Maggie stared into the closet and didn't move. Lizzie walked around her to grab a jeweled pair of flip flops. "Put these on."

"They aren't mine. I can't wear someone else's shoes." Maggie balked, stepping back towards the bed.

Exasperated, Lizzie shoved the shoes at her mother. "Please Mom, just wear them. Put them on now."

So much for fun and relaxation thought Lizzie as she watched her mother, head down, shoulders slumped, sitting on the green foot stool to change her shoes. Why can't I be nicer about this she thought. She doesn't know what is going on and I shouldn't be mean. It is just so frustrating. "Mom, give me your old ones. We'll get then fixed," Lizzie said in a softer tone.

* * *

They sat next to each other in the pedicure chairs, feet soaking in warm bubbling water. The body massager hummed and Maggie leaned her head back and closed her eyes. Thank God, Lizzie was thinking as she too closed her eyes. Soon she heard Carmella her hair stylist and nail tech say "What color today?"

"*I'm Not Really a Waitress Red* for me, as usual, and *Shanghai Shimmer* for mom. We already picked out the bottles."

Maggie opened her eyes and looking around seemed lost. The whir of hair dryers, water splashing in shampoo sinks, clients and stylists talking. Salon noise. Finally her gaze settled on Lizzie and she smiled weakly.

"Isn't this great? A foot massage and our toes painted."

Maggie nodded absently, looking down at Beth, her nail tech, gently rubbing lotion on her calves. "Feels lovely," she said.

Afterwards they both sat with their feet planted under the UV lamp drying the polish. "Let's have lunch then go to the shoe repair shop."

* * *

Lizzie had not been in Tom's Shoe Repair Shop in months, not since the stitching along the tongue of Dan's black leather wingtips started to come undone. In this day of throw away and buy new, many of the repair shops had closed. Tom's was opened in 1950 by Tom Sr. just months before Tom Jr. or T.J. was born. He grew up playing in the back room amongst the leather bits, wooden shoe forms and laces and began working after school and on weekends with his dad when he was a teenager. He went to college for design and marketing classes but never graduated. The knowledge was useful to improve the business but in reality, all he ever wanted to do was work with leather.

After his dad died in 1989 T.J. took over. He was nearly six foot tall with broad shoulders and thick black hair curling over the collar of the plaid shirts he always wore. With his faded jeans and leather boots he looked like he should be out in the woods instead of leaning over a workbench sewing a tiny pink strap on a size five Mary Jane shoe. He repaired shoes, boots, purses and belts. Plus, he designed and crafted the most glorious leather bags sold at local art shows and on-line. His creations were displayed on glass shelves in the front of his shop.

Lizzie noticed a change in Maggie instantly when the bell tinkled overhead and they walked in the door. She seemed more alert and her eyes darted about. The smell of leather was strong and there was a faint noise coming from the back room behind the counter.

"Da?" said Maggie softly as she took quick steps to the counter. "Da?" she repeated as she walked around to the archway leading to the back room.

"Mom, you can't go back there," said Lizzie as Maggie disappeared from sight.

"Can I help you?" asked T.J. looking up to see Maggie then Lizzie in his workshop.

"I'm sorry T.J.. My mom just walked right in," Lizzie said raising her hands and rolling her eyes hoping he understood there was a little something off with her. They still had not told people of Maggie's illness.

"Da?" Maggie said again as she looked around the room. "Is he here?'

The large room was bright and clean. Along two walls were work benches with tools hanging on peg board or corralled in baskets. The rich leather smell was stronger and mixed with the clean scent of polish. The third wall held shelves lined with shoes, boots and purses all tagged with the owner's name and the problem to be fixed.

"Is he here?" Maggie asked looking around.

"What are you talking about? Mom, this is T.J.. You know him. This is his shop."

"My Da made shoes. Repaired them mostly, 'cause who could afford new ones all the time," Maggie said her eyes darting about, ignoring Lizzie completely.

"This is his bench," she said as she ran her hand over

the long scared table. "Are those shoes ready to be delivered? Bridget and I can take them after school. We'll walk all over town and out to the farms if need be. Oh, sometimes we get a little something for our trouble." she said her as she smiled broadly and winked at T.J. "But mostly we just deliver the shoes. Any for Mrs. McNally? She always gives us a cup of tea and something sweet. "

Lizzie opened her mouth to talk but T.J. held up his hand. "Here sit down. I'm Thomas Jr. but my friends call me T.J.," he said as he reached out to take her hand and help her to sit. "Would you like something to drink? Glass of water?"

"Water would be lovely, unless you have tea?" Maggie said her grin growing wider.

"Sorry. No tea, just water. Tell me about your Da's shop," T.J. said as he filled a glass from the water dispenser. Bringing it to her, he pulled a stool over and sat down.

"My Da's a cobbler, a well-known craftsman," Maggie said sitting up straighter, puffed up with pride. "He had a small shop behind the house, couldn't afford to rent space in town. Didn't matter. Folks came from all over the county to have John Malone repair their shoes or if they had the money, to make a new pair. He could look at your feet and know what to do to with the leather and nails to make you walk straight and tall."

"Sounds like a real artisan," said T.J. nodding in approval.

She waived her right arm about and stated, "The gentry could go to Dublin for repairs but often came to my Da to have the sole reattached to their favorite riding boot or a seam mended on a delicate pump. The shoes looked like new when he finished. Each stitch was perfect and the shoe was shined to a high gloss."

Lizzie leaned back against the wall, shaking her head as she watched her mom sparkle with enthusiasm and charm. This is how she remembered her, this gracious lady. But now, she was being that gracious lady living in another time and place, nowhere near reality. A warm smile returned to Lizzie's face as she reminded herself to enjoy the moment.

"I see you keep a neat shop," Maggie said glancing around the tidy work room filled with tools and machines. "You have tags on the shoes. Da never did. He knew who belonged to every pair on his shelves. During busy times, like before the holidays when everyone wanted to look their best, shoes and boots would be lined up on the floor like soldiers awaiting their orders." She paused, focused on his face then asked, "Do you make much money repairing shoes?"

"Mom," cried Lizzie. "I'm sorry T.J.."

"Don't be," he said to Lizzie but never stopped looking at Maggie. "Did your Da make a lot of money?"

"Oh no, he did not," Maggie said shaking her head. Leaning closer she said in a lower voice, "Why, so many couldn't afford to pay with money. They paid with odd household bits, fresh eggs or a fruit pie." Then she broke into a huge smile and laughed, "I remember one Christmas old Mrs. Kelly brought Da a fine bone china cup and saucer with a lovely pattern of tiny pink roses and soft mint green leaves in exchange for new soles on her heavy work boots. Bridget and I were there to gather shoes for delivery when Mrs. Kelly brought it in. It was so delicate, so thin you could almost read through it." At the mention of Bridget's name Maggie touched the cross at her neck.

"Mom, I'm sure T.J. has to get back to his work," Lizzie said pulling herself away from the wall.

Maggie continued as if Lizzie had not spoken, "Da was beaming when he told us this will be your mother's Christmas present. Then he warned us not to say a word to spoil the surprise. What a Christmas morning that was," said Maggie giggling like a child. "The look on Momma's face. 'Holy Mary Mother of God. Where did you get such a lovely thing' she had said." Turning to Lizzie, Maggie said "Remember how she looked. She said she was putting it up and away for good. It was too lovely to use."

Leaning back in the chair and beaming with remembered joy, Maggie said "I'll never forget that Christmas. Da said 'It isn't too lovely to use. That is a cup for my wife to use every day. It's been kissed by the fairies and will not break.' He then turned to look at each of us children and said 'As long as it's not touched by the hand of a child.' Oh how we laughed, then Momma got up to make a fresh pot of tea and use her lovely new cup."

She looked over to Lizzie and asked, "Do you know where that cup and saucer is now?"

"Ah, no Mom. I don't," said Lizzie not sure what to say or do next.

The awkward silence was broken when T.J. said, "He sounds like a fine man, your Da."

Nodding her head, Maggie replied softly, "He was."

Lizzie opened the tote bag she had been holding tightly in her arms and pulled out the pair of sandals in need of repair. "Can you make these good as new for my mom?'

"Of course I can Lizzie," said T.J.. "I'll have them ready tomorrow."

"Thank you for your kindness," said Lizzie as Maggie sat looking around the room.

Stepping to the side TJ said, "My grandma is like Maggie. She lives in the present some, but more often in the past or in a combination of the two. It only takes a few minutes to listen to her stories. Besides I usually learn a thing or two about my family history. It's not easy, but try to make the best of the bad situation."

"Thanks again," said Lizzie smiling but she thought that's easier said than done.

Lizzie helped her mom to her feet, held her arm and headed to the car. Walking slowly she wondered why she had never heard about her grandfather's shoe repair business.

"I never knew grandfather had a shoe shop. You never talk much about your life growing up."

"It doesn't matter now. I never hear from any of them anymore."

Opening the car door Lizzie helped her into the passenger seat. "You have to buckle your seat belt."

Maggie sat looking out the front window not making any effort to secure the belt. Her hands, usually so strong and capable were lying in her lap as if they belonged to someone else.

"What's the matter Mom?" Lizzie reached over her mother to buckle the seat belt. Maggie continued to stare unseeing as if she were not in the car at all.

"What's wrong?" Lizzie asked as the climbed in the car.

Slowly Maggie turned to look at her, "I'm tired dear. I would love a cup of tea. Can we go home now?"

Lizzie drove home in silence, making a mental list of things to do to find out more about her mom. Neither she nor her brothers had gone through her parents papers. They needed to do that soon.

* * *

It was three days later when Lizzie returned to pick up the repaired sandals. T.J. was alone when she walked in. She remembered her mom's reaction to the rich leather smell and smiled.

"Hi T.J.. I came to pick up mom's sandals," Lizzie said walking through the front door.

"I have them done, Lizzie. Good as new. Let me get them from off the shelf," T.J. said heading to the back room.

Lizzie looked at the purses on display. "This is beautiful," she said pointing to a brown leather shoulder bag as she heard T.J. reenter the show room. "Your work is excellent."

"Kind of you to say. I do enjoy it."

Before she could back out Lizzie said, "T.J., I want to thank you for being so kind to my mom the other day." Without stopping to think, she continued in a rush," We just learned about her Alzheimer's a short while ago. Really haven't told people. Dad knew but didn't share." The last statement was said with a hint of bitterness. She set her purse on the counter. "I've read up on it but nothing prepares you for the reality."

"It's a hard disease. Hard for the patient. Very confusing. They know something is wrong but don't know how to fix it," T.J. said with a sympathetic smile as he held out Maggie's shoes. "Not easy for the family either. My grandma was diagnosed eight or nine years ago. She and I were real close. As you know, it takes time to come to terms with the loss of someone, but it is especially difficult when they are still with you."

"Yes, exactly," Lizzie agreed leaning forward. "We have her here, but not really." Looking up at him she sighed, "How do you do it? How do you just let her talk without correcting her?"

"Oh, that is an ongoing learning process." Placing his right hand flat on the counter he said, "I want her with me now. Listening to my plans for the shop, talking about politics, books we've read, just sharing our life. But, it's easier for her when I let her talk. I can't change her reality by telling her I'm her grandson, not her brother. That frustrates and confuses her. So I ask questions and let her talk." he said with a shrug of his shoulders.

"I have to try harder to keep my mouth shut," Lizzie said with a laugh. "Not always easy for me."

"Just listen to her. She may tell you things you didn't know about her and her life," T.J. said. "There are stories parents don't tell their children. Since she doesn't know you're her daughter she may share more, tell family secrets," he said with a wink. "Who knows what you'll find out if you just listen?"

That is so true thought Lizzie as she pulled out her wallet.

Chapter 24

To visit the Slate Run farm just outside of Tampa was to take a stroll through life from a time before Interstate highways, computers and man walking on the moon. There was electricity but only to run the lights for safety reasons and modern toilets had been installed. Several large red barns and outbuildings housed the animals and tools needed to work the fields. The white clapboard two story farm house was maintained as it would have been in the early 1900's. Hand hewn wood planks for floors and plaster and lathe walls painted white. The living room contained an old intricately carved settee upholstered in a flowered print fabric and wooden rocker. Framed photos of unsmiling people hung on the walls.

A worn multicolored rag rug lay on the floor in front of the hearth. Maggie reached down to touch it. "How did this get here?" she asked. Lizzie, who busy corralling her grandchildren, Nate and Emma, did not hear the question.

"Don't touch anything, you two," said Lizzie as the four of them walked slowly down the hall into the kitchen where two women in long skirts and white aprons were peeling vegetables.

Maggie looked around the large room then put her hands on the wooden table, looked at the women closely and asked, "Have you seen Bridget?"

"I don't know of anyone named Bridget working here," said the young girl with long braided dark hair.

"I was sure she would be here," Maggie said turning to look back down the hall.

The black cast iron stove burned hand cut wood logs to cook and warm the household but since this was summer no heat emanated from it. The open shelves were stocked with plates and bowls and jars of canned fruit. Maggie's shoulders sagged and she asked again "Have you seen Bridget?"

"There's no Bridget here," said the younger woman continuing to scrape the carrot in her hand.

"Are you sure?" Maggie asked her brows wrinkling.

"Mom, come on," said Lizzie taking her by the arm.

The older woman had been watching Maggie since she entered the house. She had seen her touch things, not out of curiosity, but as if she recognized them. With a sad, knowing smile she walked over to Maggie and said "I'm Sarah. Bridget's not here today. I haven't seen her."

Smiling Maggie said "Maybe she went to town."

"Could be," Sarah said.

"If you see her before I do, let her know I am looking for her. Thank you. Thank you so very much," Maggie said taking the woman's hand.

"I sure will tell her," replied Sarah, and then looking past Maggie to Lizzie standing in the open doorway she said, "She reminds me of my sister."

"Let's go to the barns and see the horses," Lizzie said with a catch in her throat.

Lizzie and Maggie walked through the large open barn doors together after the grandchildren had rushed ahead. The noise was muted and soft with occasional squeals of laughter from the children all around them. The floor was packed earth, littered with bits of hay. A rustling sound filled the air as small and large feet scurried about the open space. The barn smelled musty and dusty with added scent of sweat from both the humans and the animals. It was only a little unpleasant but Lizzie knew she would not want to be here too long. She was a city girl.

"Look at the horse. The sign says his name is Samuel,"

said Emma, so proud of her reading skills.

"He's so big" said Nate, eyes wide, standing on tip toe to see.

"We had a horse named Pockets," said Maggie as she looked around the large barn. Spying an old worn work bench off in the corner she raised a shaking hand to her mouth then quickly making the sign of the cross she stammered, "Jesus, Mary and Joseph. I never thought I would be here again."

"I didn't know you had ever been to Slate Run Farms before," Lizzie said turning away from the horse to look at Maggie.

"It was so long ago. It looked different but I remember the bench," said Maggie grasping tightly to the cross at her neck.

"What's the matter Mom?"

"It's not safe for us to be here. Someone will see us," said Maggie turning around to look at the people in the barn. She stared at a family with three small children scampering over the baled hay by the wall. Two younger men were leaning against the horse stall talking quietly.

"Mom, its fine," said Lizzie reaching out to pat her arm.

"No it is not," Maggie whispered turning her head quickly to the left and right all the while twisting the purse strap. "I know they are looking for me."

"Who is looking for you?" Lizzie asked in an exasperated tone.

"His family," she hissed. "Someone will tell them I'm here. If they find me it will be all over. I'll have to pay for what I did."

"You didn't do anything.' Lizzie said trying to listen to her mother and keep her eyes on the Gee kids

"I can't talk about it here. We have to leave. Now!" Maggie demanded as she grabbed Lizzie by the arm and headed for the door.

"Wait Mom. The kids are here. I have to get them."

"What kids? The kids are at home. We have to go now," Maggie pleaded, her hands trembling as she pulled on Lizzie's arm. "Hurry. They'll see us."

"There isn't anyone here. Just employees and families like us looking at the horses. Mom, settle down. Let me get Emma and Nate," Lizzie said the muscles in her shoulders tensing and her head beginning to throb.

Maggie let go of Lizzie's arm and scurried through the open barn door, the loose hay scattering around her.

"Mom, wait," called Lizzie turning to see the children staring wide eyed through the slats in the stall.

Walking over to where the placid horses stood Lizzie told the two children they were leaving.

"No Grandma, we want to stay and look at the horses," said Nate his voice rising to a whine.

"They're so big," said Emma never taking her eyes from the horse's face.

"We'll come back, I promise. Grand Maggie is tired and we need to go," Lizzie said taking each child by the hand. "Let's find Grand Maggie. Do you see her?" she asked in a light tone, trying to keep the frustration out of her voice.

Lizzie looked around the crowds of children, men and women walking the grassy area. There was an arbor covered in vines with a picnic table in the center. Two laughing children licked ice cream cones as their parents tried in vain to keep the melting mess from dripping on their shirts. A massive oak tress provided shade and held a rope and tire swing securely attached to a strong branch. Small children stood in line holding on to their parent's hand, waiting for their turn to soar.

She could not find Maggie. Fear was creeping into her thoughts. Would Maggie go far? Get hurt trying to hide? Would she fall? Lizzie wanted to call out her name but knew Maggie would be upset if she did. Maggie hated a "public scene" as she called any situation that might call attention to herself. Finally, off to the far end of the lawn, Lizzie spied her mother by another large oak tree. Maggie stood with her arms wrapped around herself and her head moving from side to side scanning the faces of the people in the yard. Her lips moved but Lizzie was too far away to hear. Trying to keep the little ones calm Lizzie pointed to the tree and said "There she is. Grand Maggie was hiding from us. Let's go over and tell her we found her."

Both children started to giggle and called out loudly, "We found you Grand Maggie. We found you."

Appearing not to hear, Maggie started to walk quickly away from the tree and towards the fields.

"Mom, wait." Lizzie called out.

Maggie never turned around. Kept walking as fast as she could, stumbling over tree roots but not falling.

Finally Lizzie hollered, "Maggie, wait for us."

At the sound of her name, Maggie stopped and turned around slowly. Her eyes darted about searching for the source of her name. She did not seem to recognize her family but stayed where she was, her hand tightly holding the cross at her neck. The children ran ahead and danced around Maggie shouting, "We found you. We found you."

"I wasn't lost." said Maggie, her voice both harsh and frightened.

"You were hiding and we found you," said Emma. "Now we'll hide and you find us."

Lizzie knelt down in front of the children, looked at them tenderly and wrapped her arms around them. She whispered to them both. "No hide and seek now. Later, okay?" With a kiss on each forehead she stood up. Looking at Maggie but speaking to the children she said "Let's go get something to drink. I'm sure Grand Maggie would love a cup of tea. And maybe, since you have been so good, some ice cream for you."

She saw the smile slowly replace the worried look on her mother's face. "A cup of tea would be lovely," said Maggie.

After loading everyone in the car Lizzie headed for the first restaurant she could find, a small diner not far from the farm. She pulled in to the nearly empty parking lot.

Looking around Maggie asked, "Why are we stopping here? I want to go home."

"Mom the kids need to use the bathroom and you could use a cup of tea."

"I can get a cup of tea at home," Maggie said sitting straight in her seat looking out the front window.

"That will take an hour and the kids can't wait that long."

"I'll wait in the car while they use the restroom," Maggie said still not turning to look at Lizzie. "I don't want to be seen."

"No. Please get out of the car," Lizzie ordered as she opened her door.

Maggie did not move. Lizzie wrenched open the back door and unbuckled the kids from their car seats. Holding both of their hands in one of hers, Lizzie wrenched open the passenger door.

"Mom, please get out of the car now. We'll get the kids an ice cream and a cup of tea for you," she commanded.

"All right. I'm getting out," said Maggie her face creased in a scowl.

Marching ahead of the others she arrived at the door of the restaurant and stopped. Lizzie came up behind her and reached for the door.

"Is it safe to go in?" Maggie asked.

"Yes, it is safe," Lizzie replied sighing deeply.

Finally settled at the table with the kids noisily eating their ice cream Lizzie looked at her mother primly seated in her chair sipping tea.

"What happened back there?" Lizzie asked.

"What are you talking about?" Maggie questioned.

"We drove an hour to show the kids this old farm and the animals. Everything was fine until we went into the barn.

You ran out of there right after we saw the horses. Who were you running away from?"

"I don't want to talk about it," said Maggie looking into her tea cup.

"Okay, not now. But, you have to explain what happened in that barn."

Maggie sipped her tea then turned to the children, "How's your ice cream?"

* * *

The drive home was quiet. The children slept in their booster seats, rocked gently by the motion of the car. Lizzie smiled as she watched them sleeping, heads to the side and mouths slightly open. Maggie looked out the passenger window all the while twisting the handle of her purse.

Just as they turned on the street for home Maggie whispered "Do you think anyone saw us?"

"Who? There were lots of people there."

"His family? Did you see any of them?"

"I don't know who he is?"

"Brendan," she hissed. "If they knew I was back they would call the Garda."

"What are you talking about?" Lizzie asked gripping tightly to the steering wheel.

"Where's Bridget?" Maggie asked her voice rising.

Sighing Lizzie said, "I don't know."

"She'll help keep them away from me," Maggie said her hand holding tightly to the cross at her neck.

* * *

Dan walked in the kitchen with a big smile and a bottle of Lizzie's favorite wine. "How about we relax a few minutes by the water?"

"Oh Dan, that would be great. Mom has gone to her

room to lie down before dinner."

"How was your day?" he asked leaning over to kiss her cheek.

Reaching for two glasses, Lizzie took a deep breath and exhaled slowly. "Fine and not fine. Scary and confusing. She took off and I couldn't find her. She's paranoid. Waiting for the family of Brendan to find her." Turning around and waving the glasses in her hands she said in a voice thick with frustration, "Oh Dan I just want things to be normal."

Dan set the bottle of wine on the counter and turned to Lizzie. He held her face in his hands and kissed her gently on the lips. "Lizzie this is your normal now. Maggie won't get better. She will only get worse."

Blinking back tears she whined, "Crying won't help. But, how can I keep her safe and me from going crazy?"

"Let's go sit down and try to figure out what we can do," Dan said as he kissed her again.

Chapter 25

The following morning, Maggie was up early. No memory of the incident at the farm remained for her, but Lizzie had been up half the night with worry. She had slid out of bed at two-thirty so her restlessness would not wake up Dan. Sitting on a cushioned lounge chair on the deck watching the moonlight reflect off the Gulf she listened to the water slap easily on the sea wall, hoping the rhythm would help her relax. Closing her eyes she fell into a deep sleep. The next thing she was aware of was the aroma of coffee and Dan leaning over her to plant a kiss on her forehead

"I'll be late tonight," he said sitting in the chair beside her. "Is Kevin or Ian coming to take Maggie today?"

"Yes. Kevin is picking her up at ten. I have to say I am surprised at how much time he is spending with her. He takes her at least once a week. She goes on calls with him. Apparently his clients love her and think more of him for spending time with her. Plus she loves the animals. She visits with the pet owners in the waiting room while Kevin meets with the doctor or staff. He said his sales go up every time she is with him," Lizzie said smiling over at Dan. "Give me a minute and I'll get you some breakfast."

"Coffee is all I need. I have a breakfast meeting with some clients at eight."

"Well I'd better get a move on so I can get Mom up and ready for Kevin," said Lizzie rising from her chair. "You know, I slept okay out here. I will remember this next time I can't sleep. The sound is soothing."

After Dan left, Lizzie went in to wake Maggie and was

surprised to find her sitting up in bed.

"You okay Mom?" asked Lizzie.

"Of course I am. Just sitting here."

"Kevin is coming at ten to pick you up."

"Why?" Maggie asked her eyes widening and her hands starting to shake. "Where is he taking me?"

"To work with him. You like to go. There are all the dogs and cats and you love talking to the people."

"Okay," she said softly. "I do like the dogs. They're well behaved and like to be petted. Are you coming too?" asked Maggie smiling and giggling like a child as she got up and walked to the closet. "I want to wear my green shirt."

"It's there. You always look great in that. Brings out your green eyes. While you get dressed I'll fix you some tea and breakfast."

"That would be lovely dear."

* * *

Lizzie had the wheat toast and jar of orange marmalade on the breakfast bar with a cup of hot tea for Maggie when she came to the kitchen.

"You look wonderful. You and Kevin will have fun today. He always takes you to a nice restaurant for lunch too."

"When is he coming?" she asked sitting on the bar stool and picking up her cup of tea. "Look at all the money," she said smiling as she peered into the cup looking at the tiny bubbles floating on the surface. "That's a good sign, you know. I should buy a lottery ticket today."

"I'm sure Kevin will stop and get you one," Lizzie said remembering the game from her youth. Whenever she and her brothers saw the bubbles in their tea cups they were certain they would find piles of money that day. Maggie used the ploy to make the children watch where they were going and keep them entertained looking for pennies on the sidewalk.

Suddenly Maggie turned to Lizzie and said, "I don't understand what happened between Danny and Bridget. We were all so sure they would get married. He was like the big brother I never had. With just us girls, except the twins, Ian and Kevin but they were babies." Maggie slowly looked down at her hands then quickly up at Lizzie. "He was so good to me during that time. I don't know what I would've done."

"What did he do?" asked Lizzie as she moved closer to the counter.

"He got me away from Kells. Oh, I know it was the aunt I ended up staying with, but I would never have made it to London if it weren't for Danny," she said holding her hand over her heart. "He risked everything to get me there. I'm sure there were troubles a plenty when he got back home. I never heard." She paused for a long time, looking up to ceiling, her fingers touching the cross at her neck. "We had plans. You know, for Danny and Bridget to come for me on their way to America. That's how I was supposed to get here. But all that changed with Sam. My Sam. He found me and brought me here."

"Why did you have to leave Kells?" Lizzie asked as calmly as she could manage.

"I don't think it matters any more. Everyone must be dead," Maggie said lowering her eyes. "But, I don't understand why I never heard from anyone again. Not in England and not in America. Why was that? Why didn't you write?" she demanded.

Lizzie knew where this was going. Her mother was confusing her with a friend from childhood. When she didn't know Lizzie was her daughter, she thought she was Meara, one of the girls who lived over the way by the Kelly's house. Or, one of her cousins or just that nice woman who let her stay in her home. She wanted to stamp her feet and holler out; I'm your daughter, Lizzie. Your only daughter, Lizzie. Knowing it wouldn't help, knowing it would only make the situation more uncomfortable, she unclenched her hands which were balled into fists at her side and pushed her feelings aside.

"I thought you could tell me what happened. Surely you heard," Maggie continued totally unaware of the sorrow etched on Lizzie's face.

Taking a calming breath, Lizzie asked again, as if for the first time, "Why did you have to leave Kells?"

"You know. Brendan." Her head dropped and she looked at her hands, twisting them in her lap. "Brendan. Brendan Taylor?" Her voice rising at the end as if not sure of his last name. "It was my fault. All my fault," Maggie said.

"What was your fault?"

"Oh, it has been so long. Sometimes I think I imagined that night." She shook her head and sighed. "My Sam knew. He knew and kept me safe. But now? Are they all dead? My sisters, my brothers, Momma and Da? I imagine they are." She inhaled softly then let it out slowly. "Dead, all dead."

"Tell me about them," Lizzie said.

"Well surely you know them almost as well as I. Kells is so small there are no secrets," Maggie said then suddenly shifting about in her chair, eyes darting around the room. "I shouldn't say more. There are secrets. You know there are."

Lizzie was uncertain how to proceed. Needing more information she pressed Maggie one more time. "Tell me about Brendan. I'm having trouble remembering him."

Maggie gazed off in the distance, watching the bright sun and cloudless blue sky. She had turned inward and didn't respond, eyes unfocused and glassy. Lizzie sat in her chair feeling alone in the room.

* * *

Maggie returned later that evening. She had spent the day with Kevin on his sales calls to veterinary clinics, ate lunch at the Casual Clam in St Pete and then dinner with him and

Becca. She came home tired but happy. "We had a great day," Kevin said as he hugged Lizzie at the front door on his way out. "I'm glad I'm taking this time with her."

"Me too Kevin. She loves being with you," Lizzie said hugging him tightly.

"Hey Lizzie, it's going to be okay. Mom's doing alright, really," Kevin said patting her on the back then taking her by the shoulders and looking her directly in the eye. "You should have seen her with the people in the waiting rooms with their dogs and cats. She was her old charming self. She is a real boost for my sales. Not that that is the only reason I take her but it is a bonus." Looking sheepish he hugged her again.

"I know Kevin," Lizzie said moving away from him. She wanted to tell him what she knew but since Maggie had not talked to him or Ian about any of this she kept silent. Why is she so different with me she wondered?

After Kevin left, Lizzie passed the open door to Maggie's room and watched as her mother sitting on the edge of the bed, eyes shut, moved her lips in silent prayer. Maggie must have felt her presence because she opened her eyes and smiled

Her disorientation and confusion was sometimes helped by routine. Since she did not go to Mass every day Maggie relied on her prayers. An old white cotton handkerchief now grey and frayed around the edges was on the bed stacked with prayer cards, leaflets and novenas. Each evening before going to sleep Maggie would take the bundle from beneath her pillow and lay it reverently on her bed, gently pulling one flap and then another. She faithfully read through each prayer.

"After all these years I know the prayers by heart. Many of the cards are so old the print has rubbed away, the paper so fragile bits fall from my hands. But darling, there is comfort in feeling the soft paper, to move these old aching fingers across the words and remember."

"Remember what Mom?" Lizzie asked leaning against the door jamb.

"Oh, who I am praying for and why. But sometimes I just don't remember. Then I pray to my Sam. He'll know who it's for. Besides, I wonder if God is even listening to me. He may not listen to me, but I know he'll listen to my Sam."

Lizzie turned away from Maggie so she wouldn't see the tears in her eyes. "Is there anything I can get for you?"

"No darling, I'm going to finish my prayers and go to sleep. I'm so tired," she said, closing her eyes and releasing a long breath.

"I love you Mom," Lizzie said.

"I love you too, darling," came the soft reply.

Chapter 26

They awoke at midnight to the sound of terrified, earsplitting shrieks. Lizzie leapt out of bed and ran down the hall to her mother's room. Maggie, sitting up in bed, her arms flailing about as if warding off some evil intruder had stopped screaming. Tears streamed down her face as she whimpered, "I'm sorry. Don't take me. I'm sorry."

"Mom you're okay. It's me Lizzie. Everything is okay," soothed Lizzie trying to sit on the edge of the bed and put her arms around her mother. Maggie, her face covered in sweat and tears, breathing hard continued to thrash about, hitting Lizzie hard in the face. "Stop it," screamed Lizzie putting a hand to her cheek.

Dan came into the room and switched on the light. "Everyone okay here?" he asked.

"No. I can't get her to stop," said Lizzie leaning back stumbling off the bed. "She hit me. I don't know if she's awake."

Seeing Dan, Maggie stopped thrashing and said, "Danny, oh Danny. I didn't mean to kill him. I'm sorry." She struggled out of the bed and pushed past Lizzie. "I didn't mean to hurt him. I didn't mean to kill him," she said in a tremulous voice, still crying and reaching for him.

"No one's hurt Maggie. No one's dead. Everyone is fine," Dan said coming to her side and putting his arms around her. "Shh. It's okay. Everyone is fine."

"He's dead. I killed him," Maggie stated, trembling and swaying slightly. "He's dead."

"No one's dead. Everyone is fine," Dan repeated.

"I can't stay here Danny. They'll find me. I'm so scared," Maggie began crying harder, huge sobs shaking her frail body as Dan held her and gently patted her back.

"Maggie no one is looking for you. I promise no one will take you away. We'll take care of you," Dan said.

Lizzie remained standing by the bed staring wide eyed at her mother as Dan peered over Maggie's head. "Lizzie, why don't you make a cup of tea for your mom? I'll help her to the family room. Maybe if we sit up for a few minutes we can all calm down. We'll get some ice for your face, too," Dan said as he continued to hold Maggie, her crying now slowed to whimpers and unintelligible murmurs.

Lizzie didn't know whether to be angry at Dan for taking her mom's side or grateful he was here to ease the situation. Holding her hand to her face tears ran down her cheeks. Not from the pain but from frustration. She could not come to grips with the disease that was robbing her of her mother. The behavior was disturbing and frightening. Maggie was still a kind and loving person but the confusion and fear she was experiencing could not be explained to her. It was causing her to be callous and crazy at times. Not that she meant to be, but she didn't remember her children, her grandchildren or even her past. There were all these new stories she was telling. People they had never heard of, events that didn't make sense, places she never mentioned before. Lizzie didn't know what to think. Her mother had killed a man? That was madness. She was tired, her cheek was throbbing now and tea was not what she wanted in the middle of the night.

Maggie sat in the family room with a tea cup in her lap, looking out the window to the blackness outside. A few lights burned on docks and homes across the canal providing a serene and peaceful backdrop to the confusing scene inside this home. She had calmed down only slightly, sitting rigidly in the chair, sipping her tea, looking lost and afraid. Pepper had taken her usual place by Maggie's feet. Lizzie didn't want to leave her alone but wanted desperately to talk to Dan. She knew that would have to wait till morning. Maggie could not be alone tonight.

Dan sat easily on the arm of the chair holding the ice pack wrapped in a tea towel to Lizzie's cheek. All the while he patted her back and said softly, "It'll be okay. It will be." Then a low chuckle escaped as he said, "Let's just hope you don't have a nasty shiner come morning. Not sure how you will explain that."

"I hope not. I don't want to say my mom took a swing at me in the middle of the night," said Lizzie leaning into him and appreciating his strength and comfortable humor. Dan could always diffuse a difficult situation with his charm and light hearted ways. Finally Lizzie said, "Dan why don't you go back to bed. You have to be up early. I'll sit here with her."

"Danny, why didn't you come for me?" Maggie asked as if she had not heard Lizzie speak.

"What was I supposed to do?" Dan asked giving her his full attention.

"You and Bridget were to come for me. Why didn't you come? Where's Bridget?"

Looking at her with tenderness he said "I didn't know where you were Maggie."

"At the woman's house. You know, the Father's aunt," frustration wrinkling her brow. "I...I don't remember her name. You left me there and never came back."

"I'm sorry Maggie," Dan said, still seated with an arm around Lizzie.

"Mom," Lizzie started but Dan squeezed her shoulder.

"Not now Lizzie," Dan said. "It's too late and she's too confused."

"I saw her. I know I did. Where's Bridget?" Maggie asked, the cup shaking in her hand.

"I don't know Maggie," Dan said as he got up and took

the cup and placed it on the side table. "I'm sorry I don't have the answers for you. Maybe we can find her tomorrow. It's late. Do you think you could sleep some now?"

"Yes, I'll try. You will help me, won't you Danny? You helped me before. Help me now. Please," Maggie begged, slumping back in the chair and lowering her head.

"Of course. You know I will. Let's get you back to bed. Lizzie will stay with you if you want," Dan said.

With that Maggie allowed Dan to help her stand and let him lead her down the hall. His reassurance and gentleness seemed to calm her down. "We'll figure it all out tomorrow. Get some sleep now."

Pepper, tail held high, padded along behind them. Lizzie walked mutely, bringing up the rear of this sad parade. Dan helped Maggie settle in the bed as Lizzie walked to the other side and climbed in under the covers.

Dan came over to kiss the top of her head. "Try to sleep honey. We can talk in the morning. Everything will look better in the morning."

With that he turned out the light and walked out of the room, leaving the light from the hall softly glowing through the open door.

"Everything's okay. Let's try to sleep," Lizzie said, doubting she would sleep at all after the unsettling events.

"Yes darling. I'm tired," said Maggie as she took hold of Lizzie's hand. "Thank you for staying with me. I don't want to be alone. Maybe they won't find me tonight."

"I love you Mom," was all Lizzie could manage to say.

In a few minutes she could hear Maggie's easy breathing and knew she was asleep, hoped she'd sleep through the rest of the night. Telling herself it would be better in the morning and there was nothing she could do in the middle of the night, Lizzie closed her eyes and slept. Not a restful sleep and she woke before six. It took a few seconds to realize she was in the guest room, lying beside her mother and not in her own room, her own bed, lying beside Dan. She got out of the bed as quietly as possible without disturbing Maggie. Pepper, who was usually meowing loudly when anyone in the household got up, sat quietly guarding Maggie's door.

"Good girl Pepper," said Lizzie as she walked down the hall to her room. Dan was awake sitting up in bed with the morning news playing out on the muted TV. Lizzie crawled in and curled up next to him putting her head in his lap. He gently stroked her hair.

"How's the cheek?" he asked. "You going to look like you were in a bar brawl?"

"It's fine. I doubt it will even bruise. What was that all about Dan?" Lizzie asked.

"She's been talking crazy for a while. Who knows what happened. Maybe it is real and maybe just movies and books getting mixed up in her head. Surely she did not kill anyone. No one gets away with murder, even back in Ireland during the war. She's just confused," said Dan.

"But she seems so sure of it. She killed someone. Someone named Brendan," Lizzie replied feeling the muscles in her neck tighten.

"So what if it's true?" he asked, softly running his hand over her back.

"What do you mean?" Lizzie asked sitting up to face him.

"What if what Maggie says is true? What if she did kill someone over sixty years ago? Do you want to turn her in? Call the police and tell them your mom has confessed to a murder of someone in Ireland, somewhere in Ireland, sometime long ago?"

"What?" Lizzie said alarm in her eyes. "No, don't be ridiculous. I don't want to turn her in. I can't believe she actually killed someone. She's so scared and confused. Panicked. Paranoid really. She is always looking around, thinking someone is about to take her away. I want to help her but don't know how."

"So, you don't think she killed this Brendan?" Dan asked his voice steady.

"I don't know Dan. She is so sure." Lizzie shook her head and touched the cheek Maggie had hit. "Her memories of growing up in Ireland are clear. Granted, a bit mixed up but still clearer than where she is now or who we are. Is it possible there was an accident and someone died?"

"I'm not sure how we could go about getting her to talk Lizzie. Or if we should. Maybe you can talk to your brothers or her doctor."

"No. We can't tell anyone else. What if... what if it's true? What if she did kill someone?" Lizzie said staring unblinking at Dan.

"Well, Lizzie I don't think... well, maybe if it is true, she could be in trouble. Though I can't imagine its true," said Dan running his fingers through his hair.

"We can't say anything to anyone. There is no statute of limitations on murder. I won't have mom spend her last years fighting a murder charge in Ireland," Lizzie said grabbing Dan by the arms. "Promise me you won't say anything."

"Hold up Lizzie. You are getting way ahead of yourself. Maggie is probably just delusional, mixing movies and books with real life. She's not a murderer. You know that. We need to talk to her to find out what happened and why she thinks she murdered a man. I just don't know how to do that. She doesn't really follow conversations. We have never been able to get her to talk on command about anything since her fall. Whatever she is thinking is what she talks about."

"So what do you suggest we do? How do we find out what happened? Dan, she probably won't remember the nightmare from last night," Lizzie sighed. Both sat silently for a few minutes then clutching the sheet tighter to her chest she started to cry. "It can't be true Dan. It can't be. Mom can't be a murderer."

"Oh Lizzie, don't cry. She's not a murderer. I agree," he said pulling her to him. "I don't know what is going on but Maggie is not a killer. I'm just not sure how to sort this all out."

Chapter 27

Dan was off to work before eight, leaving Lizzie at the breakfast bar with her coffee and thoughts. They had decided to try and talk to Maggie later in the evening when he came home though it seemed that was when she was more confused. The term for the symptom is Sundowner's. Lizzie had read on the Internet that some people with Alzheimer's become more disorientated and agitated once the sun goes down. Maggie's symptoms increased in the evening though not all the time. It was difficult to determine why she would have a good day or a bad day. Some times when others were not around she would appear lonely and sad; sitting by herself in the bedroom, not even noticing Pepper by her side. Other times, when her sons would stop by with or without their wives she might become anxious or argumentative. Yet, some evenings, she was content to sit in the family room with Lizzie and Dan watching a movie. Lizzie had not determined a pattern for the behavior. She knew it had to do with light, food and the activity level but it was still all a mystery.

Drinking the last of her coffee she turned to see Maggie standing in the entrance to the kitchen looking lost and frightened. Hair not combed and glasses askew, her bathrobe hung open revealing a thin cotton gown and a pair of black capris. Her feet were bare. Lizzie sighed loudly. She hadn't heard Maggie open the door or come down the hall. Pepper stood nearby, not making a sound.

"Morning Mom," Lizzie said smiling. The saying, fake it till you make it, ran through her head. "Sleep well?"

"I...I don't know. I'm tired but I see the sun is up so it

must be morning. I must have slept," Maggie said patting her hair.

"Would you like some tea? Maybe some toast with jam? Or, a scrambled egg?" Lizzie asked as she slipped from the stool and went to her mother. "Here, let me help you to the table. You can look out at the water while I fix your tea."

"That would be lovely dear. Just some toast and jam. Do you have that orange kind?" After she was settled in the chair she asked "Where's Danny?"

"He's at work but will be home tonight. We're spending the day together. We can go out if you want."

"No dear, I just want to sit here," said Maggie staring vacantly at the table. She picked up the cloth napkin that sat on the green woven placemat and began to twist it.

Lizzie stood in the kitchen buttering the toast, awash in hopelessness and dread. She was a take charge person with solutions to problem but now, watching her mom sitting silent and sad, the guilt and frustration began rising inside like a sand storm, blowing her thoughts this way and that. There were no easy answers, no answers at all. The knife slipped from her hand clattering loudly on the granite, bringing her attention back to the present. She gave herself a mental shake and turned to see her mom, still twisting the napkin in her hand. Talking didn't seem to help but silence only left her more alone and frightened.

"Here, Mom. Breakfast is ready," Lizzie said bringing the tea and toast to the table.

"Where's Danny?" Maggie asked again laying the crumpled napkin on the table.

"He's working. He'll be home later."

"I need to talk to him," Maggie said, barely above a whisper. "I need to see him now."

"Drink the tea. What do you need to talk to him about? Maybe I can help?" Lizzie said taking a chair across from her mom. Maggie unfolded the napkin, spread it on her lap and picked up her cup taking a small sip. The steam rose from the cup and she blew gently on the surface before bringing it to her lips again.

"He knows what happened. He can help me. I know they are looking for me," Maggie said her eyes darting about. "What if they find me?"

"Who? Who is looking for you?"

"His family. They want me to pay for what I did," Maggie hissed looking down at her hands holding the tea cup.

"Tell me. Maybe I can help," Lizzie said willing her mother to talk calmly.

Maggie looked around the room, making sure no one was listening then said, "He's dead and it's my fault. There was so much blood. It was on my hands, my blouse, my thighs. Bridget helped me clean up. They sent me away to be safe but I know they are still looking for me," Maggie said looking up at Lizzie, fear sparking in her eyes.

"Who sent you away?" Lizzie asked.

"My family. They wanted me to be safe. I wouldn't have been safe if I stayed," she said, lips quivering as she lightly touched the cross at her neck. "They wouldn't have been safe, either."

"Who were you afraid of Mom?"

"The dead man's family?" Maggie replied with steel in her voice. "Yes, they want me to pay. I should pay. I should have told what happened. I told my Sam and he said it was going to be alright. He would keep me safe but he's dead too. There is only Danny left...and Bridget. Where is she?"

Knowing she probably wouldn't answer Lizzie didn't reply to Maggie's query but asked a question of her own, "How did you kill him?"

"I don't want to talk about it," Maggie said still looking down at the tea cup. "If I tell you, you'll turn me in."

"No I won't. I promise. I wouldn't do anything to hurt you. Just tell me what you remember," said Lizzie in a voice sounding much calmer than she felt.

Maggie picked up her cup again and with shaking hands, took a sip. Setting the cup down carefully she looked at Lizzie then out to the water. "I'm scared. I was scared then. It was dark. I was waiting for someone but someone else showed up. I stuck something in him. There was blood everywhere. Then people came running and yelling. There was blood everywhere," Maggie said in a voice so low Lizzie strained to hear.

She began to gently rock back and forth in the chair, "I didn't mean to kill him. I just wanted him to go away and the other man to come. But when that man did come he screamed at me. 'You killed him. You killed him.'" Tears were running down her cheeks and she picked up the napkin and started twisting it over and over. Continuing to rock she said "So much blood. So much blood."

Lizzie stared in dismay. This was all too much to take in. She knew her mother. She was a good, kind woman, a wonderful mother and wife. The best grandma. How could she have killed someone? It had to be a dream or a movie or book or something, anything but the truth.

"It's okay," Lizzie said going to her side and wrapping her arms around the frail woman. "Don't cry. Everything is going to be alright. No one will come for you, I promise."

"Can you help me? Can you be sure they won't find me?" Maggie asked in a whisper, looking up at Lizzie, her face pale and her cheeks wet with tears.

"Yes, I'm certain," Lizzie said as she patted Maggie's back with one hand and wiped her own tears away with the other. "They won't find you. I promise I will protect you. Dan will protect you too. We won't let anything happen to you. I swear. Now eat your toast and jam. We'll sit here and look at the water and the birds. I've seen quite a few out by the boat this morning."

"Thank you, dear. I know I can trust you and Danny. I

know that. I'm sorry to be such a bother," Maggie said as she picked up the cup with shaking hands.

"You're not a bother Mom. I love you. We all do," Lizzie said trying to keep her voice even and her mind from racing as her world began to shatter like glass.

"I love you too, dear," said Maggie using the napkin to wipe her face.

After Maggie ate breakfast she moved to the family room and picked up the framed photo of Sam on the boat. Taking it with her she walked down the hall with Pepper at her side to her bedroom and closed the door. All the while murmuring "My Sam. My Sam."

Lizzie called Dan at the office. He wasn't available so she left a message with his assistant. Pacing the living room she tried to decide what to do. Dan was right. If this was all true she was not going to do anything. She didn't care what happened to some guy over sixty years ago. She didn't care if he died. All she cared about was helping her mom. She didn't know what to do or say to keep her mother calm. The disturbed sleep had been going on for a while but nothing like the nightmare from last night. She was afraid to give her anything to help her sleep for fear it would make it worse. She might end up too groggy and maybe fall if she got up to use the bathroom at night. There was no one to talk to because she didn't want anyone to know, just in case it was all real.

Chapter 28

Kevin had taken Maggie for the day. Lizzie decided to go to the condo to see if she could find information on her mom's family in Ireland. This was the day to tackle the shoe boxes filled with papers and photos in the closet. She didn't tell anyone she was going because she was afraid of what she would find. For fortification she stopped at McDonalds for a large cup of coffee but drank little as she drove, her thoughts on the task ahead.

She parked the car in the carport where her parents SUV used to be and made her way to the front door of the condo. Standing there with the key in her hand she thought, I don't want to do this. What an invasion of privacy. I would not want my kids to go through my private papers. And yet, if Daddy had shared the truth with us, I would not be doing this. Her resentment mounting, she jammed the key in the lock and entered the condo. Making her way done the hall she sipped her coffee and had to stop herself from calling out to her mom. With a shake of her head and sense of resignation she said aloud, "Get it over with Lizzie."

The louvered closet doors were open. Ian had arranged for the carpet to be cleaned and there was no trace of the bloody mess from weeks ago. Lizzie retrieved the step ladder and started to pull shoeboxes from the high shelves. She realized how easy it was for her mom to have fallen trying to get the boxes off the top shelf. If she wasn't careful she would go tumbling down.

Gabby had done a good job in organizing the boxes. The dozen or so filled with papers and photos were all to on side. Taking them two at a time she piled them on the stool at the end of the bed. Over in the corner, next to a book case was her father's reading area. A small table and lamp sat next to high backed leather chair. Carrying one box and her coffee she settled in, feeling close to her dad. His favorite books nearby and his reading glasses standing tall in the mug with the 'World's Greatest Grandpa' printed on the front.

"Oh Daddy, I wish you were here now," she sighed as she removed the lid from the box. Inside was a mix of photos, old and new. Grainy black and white pictures of she and her brothers when they were little; swinging on swings in the back yard of the home in Akron, sled riding down the hills of one of the city parks, Christmas mornings sitting amongst the toys from Santa. So many memories flooded her mind; she sat motionless and started to cry. Grieving for all that was gone; never to see her father again, never to be her mother's daughter again and never to innocently believe in the magical story of Sam and Maggie. Loneliness and longing welled inside her. For nearly half an hour she sobbed until finally, reaching for a tissue she wiped her eyes. She could cry no more. To her surprise, instead of feeling spent she found a new energy and dedication to her purpose. She would find something to solve the mystery of Maggie's past.

Realizing she could not reminisce about each of the childhood photos she quickly made a plan. Gathering the boxes she marched down the hall and stacked them on the chairs around the dining table. On the table she made piles of the items from the boxes. The family could sort through the photos at another time so those were quickly tossed to the end of the table. Bills and correspondence from businesses went into another pile. Store bought and handmade cards sat in the middle of the table.

Only once did she pick up a photo of her father and mother and not toss it quickly on the mounting pile. Maggie and Sam were on the deck of the boat gazing into each other's eyes with a look of such love and tenderness Lizzie felt the tears come again. They were an amazing couple she thought. Such devotion. Stop it Lizzie," she said aloud and placed the photo to the side to take home with her. There were many memories but now was not the time to dwell on them. Her focus was letters, post cards or notes that might explain the past.

After sorting through all the boxes she had a small stack of letters. She took them back to the bedroom and sat in the leather chair to look them over. The envelopes were yellow with age and frayed. The postage stamps foreign. Most were addressed to Miss Margaret Malone in London in her father's neat handwriting. Lizzie smiled as she held one of the envelopes knowing he had been a great letter writer just like her mom. She did not find any written to Sam which she thought was odd but maybe he wasn't able to keep her love letters as he was a soldier on the move. Her face reddened with embarrassment as she removed the letter and opened it.

Aloud she read 'My Darling Maggie, I cannot bear to be away from you. The memory of our last night...' The guilt of prying into this very private part of her parent's life made her stop reading. She folded the letter and returned it to the envelope. Flipping through the rest she found one addressed to Mrs. Matthew Charles in London. Wondering why her mother would have kept a letter written to her aunt she opened it and found another envelope. On the outside, written in a flowing script, was one word, 'Maggie.'

Lizzie leaned back in the chair. Could this be it she wondered? Could this explain the stories her mom had been telling? With shaking hands she removed the letter and read.
4 April 1943
Dearest Maggie,
I wish this was a happy letter filled with gay news of the family and town. I wish this was a letter to you on holiday in London. I wish you were here beside me. You left home three

days ago though it seems like weeks have passed. You're missed terribly. I have trouble sleeping alone as we shared a bed since we were babies. Momma carries on bravely during the day but I hear her crying at night. The young ones keep asking for you. Da has taken to his shop and works all hours. He may run out of shoes to repair.

The whole town is talking. Most are on your side. Everyone asks where you are but we haven't said a word. Father Mike has been heard telling certain folks they have enough to worry about with their own souls and not to worry about yours. He's a good man. Say an extra prayer for him. Old Father Sullivan is standing by his side, thanks be to God. The Garda respect the old priest and so far have done nothing.

Brendan is barely clinging to life. Doctor Burns said he could pass any day. He lost a lot of blood and is burning with a fever. Old Mrs. McKinney from Navin, the one who talks to the little people, put together a poultice for his wound. Only God knows if it or the prayers will save his miserable life. The wailing and crying coming from the Taylor house is a sin. That black hearted cur doesn't deserve a tear now or when he passes.

We have no idea what you are experiencing. We can only pray you are safe. I don't know if you have arrived in London but my hope is that you and Danny made it without incident to Father Mike's aunt. Being related to him, she must be a gentle woman. I know it will hurt Danny to leave you there but Father Mike says we will get this all sorted very soon. Then, Danny and I will come fetch you. God will watch over you and bring you safely back to us.

You are in our prayers. Momma has started a special novena to St Anthony. We say it in the evening along with the rosary. She says you are not lost, just missing from our sight.

Your loving sister,

Bridget.

Holding the letter firmly in both hands she leaned

forward, elbows on her knees and read it again, this time out loud. It's real; it's all real she thought. Mom killed a man, a man named Brendan.

Standing abruptly she started to pace, still holding tightly to the one page letter. How dare her parents keep something like this from her and her brothers she thought? How could they not tell them? Her dad knew. No secrets between Maggie and Sam. Everything was shared between them but not with us, Lizzie thought her anger rising. Maggie's Alzheimer's, Maggie's past. They covered it all up with their lies. "How dare you do this to me?" she bellowed waving the letter in the air. "What am I supposed to do now, Daddy? What now?

Dejected, she sat back down, the chair and surroundings no longer bringing her comfort. Tears of anger welled in her eyes and she brushed them away with her hand as the letter fluttered to the floor. She wanted to call Dan but knew he had client meetings all day. This was important but even if it was true it happened over sixty years ago. They could do nothing about it today or maybe, ever. It would have to wait till evening. Hopefully he would be home before Kevin brought Maggie back. She wanted a few minutes to talk to Dan alone about the letter and what they should do with it.

Lizzie knew calling her brothers was out of the question. They had no idea Maggie had a past. Their time spent with her was fun and carefree. They never asked questions and if Maggie started off on a story from the past they changed the subject. Ian had reminded her several times it was best to keep Maggie in the present. That wasn't true but she didn't argue with her brother. No point because he knew he was right and no amount of talk would change his mind. Then, there was the fact that she had been keeping a terrible secret from Ian and Kevin. She smiled ruefully thinking about the irony of her parents keeping secrets and her anger at them for it and her keeping secrets and how angry her brothers would be if they knew. And they were keeping Maggie's Alzheimer's a secret from the rest of the family. What was that saying she thought? Ah yes. What a tangled web we weave when first we practice to deceive.

Lizzie knew asking her mom for more details was almost impossible. Maggie ventured into the past when she drifted there of her own accord, not on command. Her fragmented memories could not be relied on though this letter did verify some of what Maggie had said. But, and this was a big but, it refuted a huge part of her history; her family wasn't dead. Lizzie began to think about questions she could ask Maggie that might bring about some answers. She would wait to talk to Dan. Between the two of them they would figure this out. For the first time in months Lizzie had a sense of control. She had found a major clue to uncover the past and help her mom. The realization brought a feeling of calm. This was not an emergency. She didn't need to go off like a crazy lady. Whatever happened was so long ago and could not be fixed now.

Surveying the mess she had created in the dining room, Lizzie went about packing the photos and papers back in the shoe boxes. She had found a marker in the kitchen drawer and identified each one. The letter from Bridget was safely in her bag. The ones from her dad she placed reverently in the night stand drawer on her father's side of the bed. She didn't know if she would ever be able to read them. Too private she thought for her or her brothers to read. The boxes were neatly stowed on the shelves and the stepstool set in the corner. Quietly closing the closet doors she smiled. Knowing a little of the truth, no matter how terrible, was better than not knowing.

Chapter 29

Kevin called to say he would bring Maggie home around nine o'clock. Becca was making dinner and their daughter, Abbey, was coming over with their kids. He told her she and Dan needed an evening alone. That was true but Lizzie thought instead of quiet time together they would be discussing Maggie. The letter she found confirmed what they thought they knew. Maggie had indeed killed a man named Brendan in Ireland and escaped to London during the war. Her family had been alive and because of the murder Maggie had never been able to go back home. And, because of that murder, they couldn't try to find her family now. As she turned the key to lock the door to her mom's condo she smiled slightly and tossed her bag on her shoulder. It had seemed like a hopeless situation, but she realized now she had answers to some of the questions Maggie had been asking. She needed to figure out the best way to use the information to keep Maggie calm and safe.

* * *

At five-thirty Lizzie heard Dan's car door slam. Walking in the front door he called out, "I'm home. Where are my two beautiful women?"

Laughing out loud Lizzie walked down the hall to meet him holding out a glass of wine. "Sorry darling, you have only me. Mom is at Kevin's for the evening."

"I like the sound of that," he said taking the glass from her hand and placing it on the hall table. Wrapping her in his arms he kissed her softly on the lips. "This is starting to be a very fine evening," he said nuzzling her neck.

Lizzie leaned back to look into the blue grey eyes of this man she loved. He had been wonderful these past months, not just tolerant but truly understanding of what she was going through. Kind and thoughtful to Maggie. Patient with her when she rambled on about the situation. They would talk about it tonight but she decided the conversation about Maggie and the letter could wait. She took his hand and led him to their bedroom.

* * *

After their tender lovemaking Lizzie lay with her head on his chest. "Will I be destroying your evening if I talk to you about Mom?" she asked.

"Of course not," he said stroking her hair. "What's going on?"

Sitting up Lizzie said, "I went to her condo today to sort through the boxes of papers and photos." A sly smile formed on her lips as she said, "I found something. A letter. A letter that explains what happened to Mom."

Now Dan sat up. "And you didn't tell me?"

Patting him on the chest she said, "This was more important. Let's get dressed and I'll show you the letter. We can put a pizza in the oven and talk."

Dan took her face in his hands and kissed her gently, "Lizzie, you never fail to surprise me, even after all these years. I love you. Now let's get that pizza going, I'm starving."

While Lizzie put the pizza in the oven Dan poured them both a glass of wine, than sat at the breakfast bar. "I can't believe you found this in all those boxes," he said waving the envelope in his hand.

"Read it aloud," Lizzie said coming over to sit beside him. She closed her eyes and let out a long breath.

All the while he read Dan shook his head in wonder. When he was finished he dropped the letter on the counter and took a sip of wine. Turning to her he said, "Lizzie, this does explain a lot. She is remembering real life. A man died and she had something to do with it. It's real." Looking at Lizzie he asked, "What do you want to do?"

"I don't know. Maybe we could show it to her and tell her he didn't die," Lizzie said reaching out to lightly touch the letter's edge.

"Isn't she going to have a lot of questions?" Dan asked putting his hand over hers.

"Like what?" Lizzie said cocking her head to the side. "This would make her feel better. She would stop being afraid that someone is coming to get her, like she is now."

"We might alleviate that fear but what other feelings would we be bringing out? If he didn't die, why didn't Bridget and Danny come for her in London? Why didn't anyone try to find her? Where have they been all these years? What happened to Liam?" Dan said reaching out to touch her face. "She is confused now Lizzie but what would showing this letter do to her? We need to think about the ramifications."

"I guess I thought this was the simple answer. He didn't die," Lizzie said picking up her wine glass. "She is so focused on Brendan's family trying to find her. If she knew he lived she wouldn't be so afraid."

"It opens up a lot more. Here she was in London with a war raging around her, the city being bombed, a young girl traumatized and alone. The man she thinks she killed didn't die. If he isn't dead, she should be able to go home but no one comes for her." In a quiet voice he said, "Lizzie, he died."

Just then the oven timer buzzed to indicate the pizza was ready startling Lizzie.

"Take it easy. Let's eat and have another glass of wine. We'll figure out what to do over dinner," Dan said rising from the chair.

Lizzie knew there were a lot of missing pieces to this story of Maggie and her past but she felt she had enough to understand most of what happened. Most but not all. Several gaping holes remained. Did Brendan really die? Why didn't anyone contact her after that first letter? Maggie had said there was only one. Why didn't Maggie contact them?

"Oh Dan, if we could only ask her. She could clear it all up. Tell us what happened and why," Lizzie groaned. "If we could clear this up she could stop being afraid."

"Clear it up for us maybe, but not for her." he said.

"Sure it would. If we could prove to her he didn't die, she wouldn't be so frightened," Lizzie offered.

"The short term memory is gone for Maggie. Even now when we tell her no one is coming to take her away, she doesn't remember. She reverts back to a time when she was afraid. If we had all the answers, I don't believe it would help her, she wouldn't remember the conversation," Dan explained.

Lizzie held her slice of pizza in both hands and took a bite. A large drop of red sauce fell from the edge and plopped onto the white paper plate in front her. "That's it. The blood," Lizzie blurted.

"What?" Dan asked puzzled.

"Mom said there was blood all over. On him and her. She also said it was on her thighs," Lizzie said putting the pizza down. "Blood on her thighs could mean only one thing."

"You think she was raped?" he asked turning to look at her.

"Yes, I do," Lizzie exclaimed reaching for her wine glass. "I knew she couldn't have killed someone for no reason. Brendan must have raped her and she fought back, somehow hurting him but not bad enough to kill him right away."

"Ok, that makes sense," Dan said nodding.

"How horrible for her," Lizzie stated her hand suddenly shaking as she set the glass on the counter. "Dan, she was just in her teens. A naive young girl. Raped and forced to leave home." Eyes shimmering with tears she leaned back shaking her head, "Poor mom. How awful."

"I agree. If she has kept this buried for all these years no wonder she can be in such a panic at times. So far the rape has not come out Lizzie and I don't think it's a good idea to bring it out," Dan said.

"You're right. But, what do we do, just keep this between us and hope for the best?" she asked her voice tight.

"No, we keep it between us and wait and see," he replied. "We can tell your brothers..."

"No, we cannot," Lizzie said emphatically. "I don't know that it helps to tell them. Mom never talks to them about anything important and she has a good time with them. Let's leave it as is. I guess just us knowing the truth or some of the truth is enough."

Chapter 30

Monday evening Dan walked through the door and dropped his briefcase on the chair by the counter. "Lizzie, where are you?"

"In the bedroom," Lizzie called out.

As he walked into the room he asked, "Where's Maggie? I need to talk to you alone for a few minutes."

"She's in her room resting before dinner."

"Lizzie I have to go out of town for the next two to three weeks."

"Now?" Lizzie asked as she spun around to face him standing in the doorway to her closet.

"Can't be helped. There are problems with the client in Atlanta."

"Someone else can go. I need you here."

"No you don't. Your brothers and sisters-in-law are here and all the kids," Dan said sitting down on the edge of the bed.

"I'm not talking about that. I need you. I need you to talk to, to be here. I can't talk to anyone else about this."

"Lizzie it's for three weeks at the most. We can talk on the phone every day. I can come back on weekends," Dan said getting up and moving towards her with his arms out stretched.

"Don't," Lizzie said as she stomped out of the bedroom. Heading down the hall for the kitchen she was startled by the sight of Maggie standing by the glass doors to the deck wearing only pink cotton capris and a white bra.

"Mom, where's your shirt?" Lizzie called out in a tone harsher than she intended.

"I don't need one today," Maggie sighed. "I looked but

couldn't find any of my clothes and besides it's warm out so I'll be fine."

"It's not fine. There are plenty of your clothes in the closet," Lizzie exploded. Everything has changed so. Before she was never without lipstick, now she's without clothes, she thought.

"Those are not my clothes," Maggie said in a loud stern voice. "I don't know who they belong to. What's happened to my clothes?"

"Sit down. I'll get you something to wear then make you a cup of tea," Lizzie said suddenly defeated, retracing her steps down the hall, stopping just inside her mother's room. "Oh Mom," she said as she looked around and surveyed the chaos. Clothes were piled on the bed, the chair and the floor. Shoes were sticking out of an open drawer. Books were scattered about. All her mother's jewelry was in a pile on the floor and the trash can was filled with a mix of pants and tops. Maggie had been so neat and fastidious about her clothes and now this. It looked like a spoiled teenager's room. All that was missing was posters of rock stars on the walls.

"Fine. Fine," Maggie answered in a soft voice and put both hands up against the warm glass of the sliding door to steady herself. Slowly she turned and walked on unsure feet to the nearest chair. Grasping the tall glass topped table she turned to ease herself down but there was no chair. She hit her head on the corner of the glass top and fell hard on the tile floor, landing on her side and smacking her head again. The glass top wobbled then fell off the pedestal, the edge slamming into her thigh, breaking the bone then landing on top of her.

"Maggie!" Dan hollered as he walked into the kitchen and watched her fall.

She lay silent on the cream tile floor with blood quickly pooling beneath her head. Small glass bits lay round her twinkling in the bright sunlight.

"Lizzie," Dan shouted. "Quick. Call 911."

Upon hearing the commotion, Lizzie was already running down the hall.

"Mom!" she screamed as she moved towards Maggie and Dan.

"Call 911 Lizzie. Do it now," Dan commanded as he knelt beside her, heedless of the blood and glass. He had moved the table top and leaned it against the door. Her eyes were closed and she was breathing softly but making no other sound. He began to pick a few tiny glass pieces off her face. Her leg is surely broken he thought as blood seeped through the pant leg. He could hear Lizzie giving information and directions to the operator. When she disconnected the call she was standing beside him with tea towels in her hands.

"Be careful Lizzie. There's glass everywhere. We can't move her. We don't know how bad she's hurt," Dan said.

"We can't just leave her on the floor. Look at this. There's glass and blood everywhere," Lizzie yelled. "Her head, her leg. My God, Dan."

"They'll be here in a minute. They'll know how to move her."

Not paying him any attention, Lizzie knelt down beside Maggie to put a cloth beneath her head.

"Don't," said Dan taking the tea towel and holding it to stem the flow of blood from the leg wound. "Get up Lizzie. You'll get blood all over yourself. Go open the door. They'll be here in a minute. Go."

Ignoring him Lizzie asked, "Mom, can you her me?"

"I don't think she can, Lizzie. She hit her head hard on the table. Just started to sit with no chair behind her. She's bleeding badly but head wounds usually do," Dan said. "I think her leg is broken too. The top hit her leg and it bleeding a lot, too.

Lizzie leaned over to inspect her mother. Blood was filling up the cloth Dan was holding tightly to her leg and more pooling around her head. She could already see the pale skin around her eyes and nose puffing up and starting to discolor.

"I'll get more towels," Lizzie said standing but not moving, just staring at her mother on the floor.

"Go Lizzie. The ambulance is here," Dan said as the loud wailing of the sirens penetrated the walls.

The scene was even more chaotic than before. Five EMT's entered the house with a stretcher and all manner of equipment.

"My name is Steve Miller. Can you tell us what happened?" The tall dark haired man with a clipboard in his hand asked Dan as the others tended to Maggie.

"My mother-in-law fell. She went to sit down but there was no chair. She hit her head on the table there. The glass top came off and landed on her. I think it may have broken her leg. She hit the tile hard. Her head was bleeding, a lot. We tried to stop it but there was a so much blood."

"She's not fully dressed," Steve stated.

"The situation has deteriorated recently," Dan replied. "She has Alzheimer's." He was hoping he would not need to explain further but the stoic look on the man's face told him he should. "She forgets things, gets mixed up and confused. My wife and I were in the bedroom talking and Maggie was supposed to be in her room resting. She fell as I came into the room. I couldn't get to her in time." He ran his fingers through his hair and looked around for Lizzie.

"Does she live with you?" Steve asked.

"Yes with my wife, Lizzie, and me. She still has a condo on the beach but she stays here."

"Has she fallen before?"

"Yes, several times but she has been okay. Some bruises, never broke anything, hasn't hit her head. Well, she did fall several months ago and was taken to Largo Medical. They didn't keep her. It wasn't bad," he said seeing Lizzie standing alone in the kitchen.

As Dan continued to talk the other EMT's worked with

Maggie. A cervical collar was placed around her neck and a back board was used to pick her up and place her on the gurney. Her body was limp. She was breathing but not moving. One EMT was dealing with her bleeding leg and another, the gash on her head. Chunks of glass were tossed to the floor as they wiped blood from her around her eyes and took her vital signs. Oxygen was administered with a mask.

A lovely red headed woman with a name badge that read Bridget came over to Dan. "Steve, I was with the team that picked her up last time." Turning to Dan she said, "My name is Bridget. Maggie talked to me like she knew me. I had never met her before but I was able to calm her down. I don't think I will be of much help in that regard today. She's unconscious. I know your wife was upset that day. This is a difficult disease. I'm sorry."

Dan smiled weakly and said, "Thanks. We're doing the best we can under the circumstances. Maggie spoke of you a lot, as if she knew you. She had a sister named Bridget and you reminded her of her. It has caused some confusion around here but we were grateful you were there that day."

"Glad I could be of assistance," said Bridget as she turned and walked with the gurney out the door.

Lizzie hovered nearby leaning on the kitchen counter with her arms wrapped around herself, crying quietly. She couldn't look at the floor with all the blood. She wanted to go to her mother, lying so still on the gurney, but she was unable to move. This can't be happening, she told herself. Not now. Please not now. Maybe that redheaded EMT, that Bridget, could get Maggie to wake up, to be okay. She started shaking as she thought of the first time she saw Maggie on the floor covered in blood. That horrible day she was told of Maggie's Alzheimer's. The day her world was altered forever.

Dan finished talking to Steve then walked over to Lizzie. "They are taking her to Largo Medical. You can ride with them or I'll drive you over. As soon as they leave I'll call your brothers. Lizzie, we don't know what is going on yet," said Dan as he wrapped her in his arms. Lizzie laid her head against his chest and began to tremble, gasping and sobbing, unable to control herself. Holding her tightly he let her cry, saying, "It's okay, honey. There, there, baby."

"I can't go with her," Lizzie finally said into his shoulder, her voice hoarse from crying.

Patting her back Dan said "No problem. We'll go together." Then he turned to Steve who stood on the other side of the counter, "I'll take my wife to the hospital after you leave. Thank you for everything."

Dan and Lizzie stood in each other's arms for several minutes after the EMT's left with Maggie. Her shaking had subsided. The siren had faded and the house was quiet.

"I don't know what happened to me just now. I couldn't deal with it all. What if you hadn't been here?" asked Lizzie.

"Lizzie, you would have been fine," said Dan taking her by the shoulders and looking in her eyes. "I was here so you didn't have to be in control. That's alright you know. But you would have been fine. You have handled a lot of things with the kids, your job and your mom. You'd have done great."

"Great?" Lizzie asked regaining her composure and wiping her face with a tea towel from the counter. "I shouldn't have left her half dressed in the kitchen. If I'd taken her with me to the bedroom she wouldn't have fallen. I told her to sit down. It's my fault this happened," Lizzie said her jaw tight.

"Stop it right now Lizzie. Don't go there. You have told her to sit down hundreds of times before and she found a chair to sit in. This is not your fault. This disease is taking over her mind and we can't change that."

Wrapping her arms around him she let out a long breath and leaned into him. "You're right. I know it but in my heart I feel..."

"Well just don't Lizzie. This is not your fault. Not anyone's fault. Come on. Let me call your brothers and get to the hospital."

Chapter 30

Lizzie sat by the bed trying to concentrate on the book in her lap when she noticed a slight noise, a change in breathing. Looking over at Maggie, thin and frail under the stark white sheet, she stood up to stretch her aching muscles. The molded green plastic visitor chair had not been purchased for comfort she thought arching her back and rolling her neck from side to side.

Shoving her hands in the pockets of her black cargo pants she stepped beside the bed. There were no machines attached to Maggie, no blinking lights to signal all was okay or there was a problem. Several years ago Sam and Maggie had both signed Do Not Resuscitate orders for situations like this. Lizzie missed the hum and throb of them. The gentle rhythm of life. She wondered how many people have watched those machines and prayed for them to continue? How many have prayed for them to stop? I want my mom back she thought reaching over to hold her hand, so small and fragile.

Maggie's room was at the end of the corridor. Not a lot of traffic outside the door. Lizzie could hear the conversations of the nurses, respiratory therapists and doctors as they went about their work, not unaware of the tragedy swirling around but somewhat hardened to it. "Where do you want to go to eat? Did you stop at the Fresh Market in the square last Thursday? How was the date last night?" Normal conversations, the world continuing to go on in spite of what was occurring in this pale green room with the sun peeking through the slatted blinds.

Maggie, in the hospital for two days since the fall in the

kitchen, had not regained consciousness. The test had revealed a slow bleed in the brain. Surgery could be done but at her age and with Alzheimer's, the family decided to do nothing but wait and see.

Everyone had come by to see Maggie. The Gee Kids, Phyllis, T.J. and other friends. People who knew Maggie and Sam from the condo, church, bingo and the beach. They didn't stay long, just came in, hugged the family and said, "We will keep her in our prayers."

"So many people are praying for you, Mom. Can you feel all that love coming your way?" Lizzie had said still holding her hand.

The room was filled with flowers she could not enjoy and cards she could not read. Happy pictures drawn by the Gee Kids were taped to the wall. The picture of Sam on the boat wearing his captain's hat sat on the bedside stand. Ian and Kevin had been by her bed most of the time but it was Lizzie who refused to leave. Finally, in the early hours of the morning Dan had convinced her to come home for a shower and to sleep a bit. The doctors did not expect anything to happen right away. Maggie was holding her own, in a coma.

It was midafternoon when Lizzie had returned to the hospital, stopping just outside the door to her mother's room. Kevin and Ian were sitting on each side of the bed, holding Maggie's hand and talking softly to her.

"We love you Mom. You have been here for all of us whenever we needed you. We could not have asked for better parents. You and Dad were the greatest," Kevin said in a shaky voice.

"We want you back Mom," said Ian, his soft voice filled with despair.

Barbara, the day nurse, making her rounds came to the door then. "Hello Lizzie. Feeling better after a shower and a nap?" she asked smiling.

Kevin and Ian turned to look at Lizzie with red eyes

and wet cheeks. Both women walked into the room. "How's she doing?" asked Barbara.

"No change," said Ian, patting Maggie's arm.

"I'm glad you went home Lizzie. You look better. Dan made you eat and sleep?" asked Ian standing to give his sister a hug.

"Yes, he made lay down for a bit and eat. I didn't sleep much but must have dozed some. I do feel better. He even took my phone so no one could reach me. Has anyone else been here?"

"Becca came by and so did Rose. They stayed for a bit and will be back tonight," Kevin said. "I think the word has gotten out about her condition. There haven't been any of the friends dropping by like yesterday.

"If you boys need to leave I'm fine here by myself. Dan will be over shortly," Lizzie said.

"I do have a few things I need to do," said Kevin.

"Me too," said Ian. "We'll both be back in a couple of hours.

Lizzie hugged her brothers and assured them she was fine alone. "I have a book to read and I brought coffee. I'm good."

Barbara finished checking Maggie's vital signs just as the brothers were leaving. She turned to Lizzie and said "I'm sorry for what you are all going through. From what we have seen here your mom must have been an amazing woman. Well loved by her family and friends. It's nice to see that. I know dealing with an Alzheimer's patient is not easy."

Lizzie's eyes filled with tears and she reached into her pocket for a tissue. "She was great. She and our Dad. They were quite the pair. She's been lost without him."

"Has he been gone long?" asked Barbara.

"He died in April. We found out about the Alzheimer's shortly afterwards. She was diagnosed three years ago but they didn't tell us."

"Not unusual honey. Many people don't want to admit it. They figure they can manage just fine and they do, until they can't. I'm sure you took good care of her," Barbara said as she turned to leave.

"This is my fault," Lizzie said in a rush. "I should have been watching her more closely."

"No honey, it's no one's fault. It's life. You do the best you can, that's all anyone can do," Barbara replied in a soothing voice.

"You don't understand. I left her alone in the kitchen. If I had taken her with me to the bedroom, this wouldn't have happened," Lizzie said, shaking her head and tears streaming down her face. "It's all my fault."

"No it's not. It just may be her time. Maybe she wants to be with your daddy," said Barbara with a reassuring pat on her arm. "You stop blaming yourself. From what I have seen you are a wonderful daughter. You won't help yourself or anyone with those thoughts running round in your head. Listen to me. I've been a nurse for over twenty-five years and I can tell when there is goodness and love in a family. And you all have that for sure. Now you just sit there and read that book you brought. Give yourself a break, honey."

With that she left the room and Lizzie sat in the chair by Maggie's bed. Instead of picking up the book she reached for Maggie's hand. She held it for a long time then said, "I love you Mom. I know you have been through a lot lately. I want you here but if you want to go, want to be with Daddy, that's okay. We will all be fine. You taught us well and loved us fiercely. There is no doubt about that." Then Lizzie laid her head by Maggie's arm and cried. Cried for all the wonderful times they shared and all the time they would not have together. She knew her mom was not going to wake up. Feeling the warmth of Maggie's skin and the wetness of tears on her cheek, Lizzie finally began to forgive herself for the fall. She knew Dan was right and this was not her fault.

Dan found her this way, crying softly and clutching Maggie's hand. "Hey honey. It's going to be okay," he said wrapping his arms around her and bringing her to her feet. "I'm so sorry Lizzie. I wish it was different but here we are. You know she has been lonely without Sam. And, so confused. Maybe this is for the best. They'll be together."

Holding tightly to Dan, totally lost in her sorrow she cried. All the while he patted her back and murmured "There, there, honey. There, there." When she felt she had no more tears she leaned back and looked into his eyes. A smile came to her lips and made it all the way to her red, wet eyes. "You know those are magic words," she said sniffling.

"Really?" he asked smiling down at her. "How so?"

"When Mom would be sad, Daddy would hold her tight, pat her back and say, 'There, there honey.' It always brought her back to us smiling. Remember on the fourth of July at the fireworks. She said that is what he said to her when they met."

"So she did. We may never know what really happened with Maggie. Are you going to say anything to your brothers?"

"No. I've thought about it and you are right. No point in casting a shadow on her and Daddy. We don't know the whole story," she said sniffling.

The doctor came in for his afternoon rounds. After checking on Maggie he turned to Dan and Lizzie and said, "I can't say for sure how long she has but if your family wants to come say their goodbyes, I suggest you do that now. It could be a few hours or at the most, another day."

Dan had his left arm around Lizzie and reached out with the right to the shake the doctor's hand. "Thanks. We appreciate you telling us. I'll make the calls."

* * *

Ian, Rose, Kevin and Becca arrived the same time as

Father Mike. He performed the last rights, Anointing of the Sick, for Maggie, his most ardent parishioner, wet eyes. When he was finished he took a small object from his pocket and placed it on the pillow next to her head. "Here's a medal of St. Jude. You know, Maggie, you were never a lost cause."

Slowly the rest of the family arrived. With so many people, they could not all fit in the room. The night nurse, Sarah, made arrangements for them to use an empty room down the hall. As the evening wore on all the Gee Kids and Great Gee Kids came in to tell Maggie they loved her and thank her for being their Grand Maggie. Each one leaned over the rail of the hospital bed to plant a kiss on Maggie's cheek or forehead.

As many of the grandchildren had little ones to tend to they gave hugs all around and headed for home. There were lots of tears and promises to call if anything changed. By midnight only Maggie's three children and their spouses remained. The conversations around her bed were sad and funny and filled with stories of their childhood. Most had been repeated at family gatherings but a few were ones only they knew. Moving around the room they sat together or apart depending on their emotions at the time. As Lizzie sat by the bed, holding Maggie's hand she noticed her breathing slowed. Calling the others to gather round they took Maggie's hand or touched her arm. All wanting to be with her at the moment she was gone, all wanting her to know she was loved deeply. Finally her breathing ceased. No one moved for several minutes then Sarah entered the room.

The nurse checked her for a pulse and turned to the family and said, "I'm sorry. She's gone."

Chapter 32

"Lizzie, may I please speak to you?"

The caressing tone of the Irish brogue calling her name caused her to smile and turn slowly around. In front of her stood a tall, thin elderly man with a full head of slivery grey hair and sharp blue eyes. He was well dressed in a dark blue suit with a fresh white shirt and red tie. She had seen him earlier at the church

"Lizzie," he said again as he reached for her hand. "I am so sorry to be meeting you like this, at this sad time. My name is Danny, Danny Callahan. I'm your uncle, by marriage of course. I am married to your Aunt Bridget. She's sitting over there." He pointed to the pretty woman she had seen with him at the church. "Oh, if only we had known Maggie was alive, if only they both could have been together," he said, still holding her hand with both of his, shaking his head from side to side.

He stopped talking as Lizzie took a step back and then said softly, "My dear, I can see I've upset you."

Dan was keeping a close eye on Lizzie. He wanted to protect her from everything, even the sadness of death. As he watched from across the room she was smiling, reaching out to shake hands with an elderly grey haired gentleman. The smile disappeared and was replaced by a look of wide eyed shock and bewilderment. Within in few long strides Dan was beside his wife with an arm wrapped around her.

"What's going on?" he demanded.

"Ah Dan, I did not mean to upset our Lizzie."

"Our Lizzie?" Dan shot him a look of confusion then

turned to Lizzie.

"I didn't know how to introduce myself and I didn't do it right. Let's get her over to the sofa for a sit. My name is Danny, Danny Callahan. I'm married to Maggie's sister Bridget. She's right over there."

"Honey, here, sit down." Dan guided her to the sofa, keeping his arm around her and holding tightly to her hand. The announcement that Maggie's sister, Bridget, and her husband were in the family room, though spoken softly, was enough to bring the room to a hesitant hush. The abrupt change from solemn lowered voices to complete silence brought a worried looking Ian and Kevin from the kitchen.

"What the matter Dan?" boomed Kevin as if the volume of his voice would keep any additional sad news at bay.

"Take it easy Kevin," said Ian as he strode toward his sister sitting next to the two older people on the sofa.

"Hello. I'm Ian Murphy."

Danny started to get up but Ian protested. "No sir. Please, stay seated."

"Well then, I'm Danny. Danny Callahan."

"Mom's Danny?" Ian and Kevin asked together.

"I'm not sure, but I would venture to say yes. This is your Aunt Bridget, my wife, Maggie's sister. Ah, if only the two girls had seen each other again. All these years we believed she was gone, believed our Maggie died so many years ago and never had a real chance to live. And now, look at all of you. Oh, thanks be to God, Maggie did have a life and a good one from what we can see. Ah, there is so much to know. How did all of this happen? We thought she was dead all these years." Danny's head dropped and his shoulders sagged from the weight of his words. He turned to his wife, who had not spoken and took her hand. "I'm so sorry Bridget."

People from other parts of the house and the deck began to quietly crowd around the family room as best they could. Everyone wanted to hear.

Dan broke the spell, "Please give us some space. Please."

Becca came to the rescue and began herding people out of the house and on to the deck. "Let's give them some time together," she said. "There's plenty to eat and drink. Help yourselves."

All three of the children were staring at the woman, their Aunt Bridget, who looked remarkably like their mother. The same green eyes and warm smile. No one said a word for several moments and then the two brothers spoke at the same time.

"Where have you been?" asked Ian.

"How did you know Mom had died?" asked Kevin.

"We're here on holiday. We come to this area almost every year. We've been so close and never knew. I saw the obituary in the paper. The photo of Maggie, Then and Now. Bridget recognized her right away," Danny said squeezing his wife's hand. "It's an odd pastime I know but we read the obits every day, no matter where we are. When we saw Margaret Mary Malone Murphy of Kilcoty Ireland we were intrigued. I thought we might be wrong because she was from Kells, but Bridget was insistent it was our Maggie. We decided to come to the Mass. If it wasn't our Maggie, we would remember her and say a prayer. And here we find it was our Maggie," Danny sighed and looked at the three grown children. "It is a day of great sadness and joy," he said.

Lizzie's sat forward and turned to face the couple, her face twisted with anxiety and asked in a solemn voice, "What happened in Ireland?"

Bridget, who had been staring at the two brothers, sighed deeply, looked at Lizzie and spoke for the first time, "It was a long time ago and we haven't talked about it for years. We talk of Maggie often but not of those days."

Just then Rose came in carrying a tray with tea and coffee. "How about we let Uncle Danny and Aunt Bridget have a cup of tea as they talk. I'm Rose, Ian's wife," she said placing the tray on the table. "Do you need anything else?" she asked.

"Tea is just lovely dear," replied Bridget.

The lilt in her voice and the way she said lovely cause everyone to smile.

"You sure sound like Mom," said Ian with an amused grin.

Rose took a seat by Ian and Becca arrived to sit opposite Kevin. After everyone was settled Danny spoke again, "I'm sure you have as many questions for us as we have for you. If you would indulge an old couple we would appreciate it if you could tell us about Maggie and her life. We heard such wonderful things during her Mass but maybe you can share a bit more."

Ian was the first to speak up and tell the story they all knew about Maggie losing her family in a fire, going to London, meeting their dad, and then coming to America. "She had a good life, she was happy until Dad died and... well, we found out about the Alzheimer's. Things were difficult these last months. But, before that it was good. All good," he said wiping his hands on his thighs.

Lizzie looked at Dan for support and he squeezed her hand and nodded. Speaking softly she said "That's not the truth. She lied to us all these years. She wasn't even from Kilcoty. The stories she told recently were the real truth." Reaching to her throat and touching her mother's cross that she now wore around her neck, she continued. "She didn't talk to you boys the way she talked to me and to Dan. She told us things...she said she killed a man in Kells."

Ian and Kevin turned to her, eyes and mouths wide open.

"Lizzie, are you crazy? Mom didn't kill anyone," said Ian jumping to his feet.

"What is wrong with you Lizzie?" asked Kevin in

disgust, is hands clenching in his lap.

"Take it easy you two," Dan demanded. "Hear her out."

Rose took Ian's arm and guided him back to his seat.

"She told me she did. At first I thought she was mixing up life with movies or books she had read. It all sounded so crazy but she was afraid, terrified at times. The nightmares, the crying, the fear. I found the letter you wrote to her in London," she said pointing to Bridget. "She ran away from Ireland after killing a man and Dad rescued her. Not like the fairy tale they told us. He knew what she did. They never told anyone. Maybe now we can get the whole story," said Lizzie her eyes bright with determination and a flush on her cheeks.

Everyone remained silent, trying to make sense of what Lizzie had just blurted out.

"Ah Lizzie, it isn't so bad as you think," said Bridget, taking her hand. "Brendan didn't die."

"What?" Lizzie gasped.

"He was an awful cur and should have but he didn't die until a few years ago. And it wasn't the wound Maggie gave him that did it, but lung cancer," replied Bridget patting Lizzie's hand.

"And Liam? What happened to him?" asked Lizzie.

"Who is Liam?" Ian and Kevin asked in unison.

"He was the fella your momma was sweet on. Brendan's brother," Danny said with a gentle smile. "He grieved for his lost Maggie for some time. The grief and guilt nearly killed him. But time worked its magic and a few years after the war he met a nice girl from Naven and was married for years until they both died in a car accident some time back. God rest their souls. We were all good friends."

"Will someone tell us what is going on here?" demanded Kevin.

"I suppose we should have Bridget tell us the story," said Danny putting his arm around her.

"It was so long ago," said Bridget. "And, yet I remember it so clearly."

Chapter 33

"We two girls were in our own world with plans for the future. I was almost 18 and Maggie just 10 months younger. She was the adventurer. The one who spoke up to the sisters at school or old Pastor Sullivan"

Lizzie broke in, "Pastor Sullivan? Mom refused to go to confession to Father Sullivan a few weeks ago. She must have thought it was the same man."

"Maybe she did. She never liked him. He would tell us a good and proper dream for an Irish Catholic girl was to get married and raise a family. Not our Maggie. Oh she wanted a family for sure, but she wanted to be a writer. Write wonderful stories that everyone wanted to read. To go to America and have people know the name Margaret Mary Malone," Bridget said proudly.

"Our parents, John and Mary Malone, worked hard to keep our small family alive in those difficult times. Da was a cobbler, had a small shop behind the house. Momma was busy with all of us children. The spare shop was neat and organized. Thick walls whitewashed clean and the dirt floor so hard packed a nail bounced when dropped. Maggie and I delivered the shoes.

"Even back then Danny was my fellow," she said, smiling and patting his hand. "We would be married as soon as I turned 18. Our parents were happy to have the oldest of their daughters get on with her life. Not because it would be one less mouth to feed but because it was time and Danny was a grand fellow.

"We all knew Liam Taylor had his eye on Maggie. She

knew it too and felt the same way. But, for all her outspokenness she was shy around Liam. Her cheeks reddened and the well planned words would not come out of her mouth when she saw him in the shop owned by his father, Big John Taylor. A tentative hello was all she could manage. Liam took after his father in looks and temperament. A good, kind man.

"Brendan, Liam's older brother by eighteen months, favored the father in looks and size too but not in any other manner. His black heart was hidden by a handsome face and a hearty laugh. No grocery shop for him, he chose to work in the Roaring Horseman, the bar across the street owned by his Uncle Martin. He had an eye for Maggie but not the way his brother did. He wanted to take her down a peg, show her she was no better than any other lass in town.

"That day, that awful day," Bridget stopped and shook her head. "We haven't spoken of it for so long."

"We know this is not easy for you but please tell us what happened," Lizzie pleaded.

"Of course dear," replied Bridget taking a deep breath and letting it out before continuing. "Liam asked Maggie to go for a walk later in the evening. She happily agreed but wanted Danny and I to go along. We would all meet down the lane by the O'Brien farm at half past eight.

"Ryan and Molly O'Brien moved to America the year before and left the small plot of land. A fire had ravaged the home, killing his entire family. They had been spared because the two had gone to visit her sick mother in Navin. The roof and several of the walls was gone from the main house. The barn, though not destroyed by the fire, no longer had a roof. No one had the money to buy the farm and no one wanted to rebuild on the sorrowful land so it stood empty except for the occasional night visit by one of the locals who'd been drinking too much and his wife wouldn't let him come home.

"After the evening meal we girls went to the room we shared with our younger sisters to get ready. I remember

Maggie using our momma's ivory handled hair brush to tame her curly black hair and put on the long sleeved white blouse and a pale blue skirt she wore for Mass on Sunday." Bridget's brightened as she added softly, "I remember how pretty she looked."

Turning to Lizzie she said "A light misting rain was falling as we walked arm and arm down the lane, the full moon providing the light. Danny was early. We offered to stay and wait for Liam but Maggie shooed us off." Darkness fell over Bridget's face and she tightened her grip on Danny's hand.

"Bridget, my dear, we couldn't have known what would happen," he said putting his arm around her thin shoulders. "After all these years you know that."

With a tight smile Bridget nodded and continued, "When we had gone over the hill out of sight, Brendan appeared. He had been lurking in the shadows of the barn waiting for Maggie. He told Liam she had left a message that she would be late because she was delivering shoes for our Da." She was silent, turning to Danny, shaking her head she said softly, "I can't say it."

Pulling her closer to him Danny said in a low voice, "Maggie tried to fight him off but he was too big, too strong. It was a terrible thing to have happen to such a sweet young girl."

"My God," cried Ian, looking as if he had been punched. Turning to face Lizzie he asked, "You knew about this, too?"

Dan tightened his arm around her shoulder and answered, "No, we didn't know. Whatever Maggie said was mixed up and we couldn't determine what was real and what wasn't."

"But you guessed?" demanded Kevin his face flushed with anger.

Becca stood and walked over to put her hand on Kevin's shoulder. "Listen to yourselves. What difference does this make? This is about Maggie, not you. The only way it relates to you is finding out what happened to her and maybe that will help you understand why she was the way she was. But even so, it is not about you. So please, let Uncle Danny and Aunt Bridget tells us about Maggie."

Lowering his head Kevin said, "Okay, you're right. Sorry Lizzie, Dan."

No one said anything else. With a sigh Danny continued, "When she told him she was going to tell everyone what he had done he became angry and threatened her. Maggie looked about for any stray tool to use as a weapon when she saw the old rusted railroad spike on the wooden work bench. Grabbing it she thought she would use it to scare him away. But as he came at her again she plunged it into his stomach. Brendan grabbed the end and pulled it out. Just then Liam rushed through the door to find Brendan falling to his knees. He saw the blood and heard Brendan screaming 'She tried to kill me.' Liam said he never forgave himself for that awful decision when he believed his brother and turned on Maggie.

"We heard the commotion and came running from the far side of the hill. Could see Maggie standing in the doorway. Heard Liam yelling for help. When we reached her we saw the blood on her hands and clothes, her hair loose and wild around her face, eyes wide with terror. She tried to tell us what happened but there was too much confusion. The Ryan brothers from down the road heard the noise and came running to the doorway. Old Mr. and Mrs. O'Shay were coming back from town in their horse drawn cart and stopped on the roadside. By then, Brendan has passed out from shock and blood loss. Liam, still kneeling over Brendan was yelling, 'You've killed him Maggie. You've killed him.'

Looking down at his hands, holding tightly to Bridget's, Danny said, "It was so long ago yet seems like yesterday. Our Maggie has always been in our thoughts and prayers, every day."

"What happened to her?" asked Ian his voice husky with emotion.

Bridget, sitting up straighter, seemed to be gathering her inner strength when she said in her lilting brogue, "We know you have questions and we want to answer them, but let us finish the story and then..."

"'Tis a good idea," said Danny.

Bridget continued, "Danny sent us home. Da and Momma were so upset when we arrived, seeing Maggie covered in blood. I told them what I knew and that Danny would be back with more news. Ma and I took Maggie into the room we shared to clean her up. She was whimpering and shaking as if she had been out in the cold without a wrap. She didn't want Ma there because of what had happened. I didn't know then, not until I helped her remove her skirt. Ma offered to bring us tea and I can still see the hurt and fear on her face as she left the room." Bridget closed her eyes and sighed. "When I saw the dried blood on her thighs I knew. I wrapped her in my arms and rocked her. All she said over and over was 'Don't tell'. God help us, if we had only known what a few weeks would bring."

Danny crossed his legs and leaned back, "When I got to the house John and Mary were in the kitchen. John pacing and Mary on her knees by the hearth with a rosary in her hands. I told them what I knew, that Brendan claimed Maggie came on to him, teasing and offering herself. I had to tell him what I knew. It would be all over town by morning." Looking around at the faces of Maggie's children, he faltered. "This is hard to tell but you must know the truth now. Brendan had come to for few minutes and called her a wild woman. Lord, she was no wild woman, she was just a child. He said she told him to take her to America as the families would have nothing to do with them when this got out. He claimed she attacked him because he wouldn't promise to take her away. That's what he told Liam. That's what he told everyone...Maggie tried to kill him."

Bridget broke in, "Everyone knows Maggie would never do such a thing. She didn't care a whit about Brendan. It was Liam she had eyes for not Brendan,"

"We had to get Maggie away. There was a war on. If we could get her to London she could get lost in the city," said Danny. "The Taylors were a powerful family. Brendan was dying. To them she was a murderer. It didn't matter that Maggie was... was raped." He closed his eyes and sat silent as the others watched him intently, then continued, "I ran to the Rectory at Saint Colmcille's knowing old Pastor Sullivan would be sleep and Father Mike would be in the kitchen at the back. Father Mike was grand. Had been in the parish for five years and got along with all the members but mostly with the little ones and the young adults. We had become friends, a rare thing for a priest to have. Everyone thought the priests walked on water like Jesus Christ so it was difficult for them to find a person to talk to about fishing or a good book.

"The back door was open so I knocked on the wooden jamb and stepped inside. Father Mike was sitting in his straight backed chair at the long wooden table. I can see it so clearly. In front of him was a bright lantern, a steaming cup of tea and an open book. I must have looked a fright because before I could say a word he pushed back the chair and was on his feet asking, 'What's wrong?'

"We ran across the fields lit by the same full moon that only hours earlier had been romantic but then looked ominous casting shadows about. I told him what I knew and we decided on a plan to get Maggie to London. Both John and Mary knew Father Mike would fix it, he was their only hope. We drank cups and cups of tea as the details were laid out.

"It was one of the worst nights of my life," sighed Danny. "Telling those poor folks we were taking their young daughter away to England in the middle of a war. Why, none of us had ever been further than Dublin in our lives, except for Father Mike. He told them about his Aunt in London.

Everyone agreed it was best.

"The plan was to leave early in the morning, get her to Dublin where there was sure to be a boat headed for London. With the war going on she'd be able to mix in with the other Irish girls going to work in the factories. I offered to go with her to get her settled."

"I wanted to go, too," said Bridget. "But they would have none of it. Just when it was all decided, Maggie came out of the bed room looking so frightened. Her hair wild and her face pale. Da went to her, held her close and said "There, there, it'll be alright.'

Lizzie looked at Dan with a knowing smile and repeated, "There, there."

"Father Mike was the one to explain the plan to her. We never knew that would be our last night with Maggie," Bridget said turning to look at Lizzie. "Maggie's few clothes were put into a leather satchel with a fine sturdy strap made for her by Da. He had made one for each of us knowing one day we would head off to America. He told her the bag was a piece of him to carry with her where ever she went."

Lizzie gasped thinking of the leather bag her mother kept under the bed. "I asked to use it once when I was a teenager," she said. "Mom said no, it was a special bag and I dare not touch it. I remember I got angry with her. I hadn't thought of it in years."

"Your grandda made it. It was special," Bridget said smiling. "Momma pulled the delicate rosary beads from the pocket of her apron and put them in Maggie's hand. She told her to pray with them every day. I took the tiny cross on a gold chain, the one you are wearing now, that Danny had given me the Christmas before off my neck and put it on Maggie's. She protested but I told her she could give it back when this was all over. The little ones were in their beds so she kissed them as they slept and left the house."

Danny leaned forward in his chair and said, "Father

Mike had secured a faded and worn cart drawn by an equally faded grey mule from Mr. Wylde. He was indebted to the priest for helping his youngest son, Sean, get passage to America two years before. By then Sean had a fine job in Boston working in a factory and was sending money every month to help support the family. Even though it was just past dawn the farmer had been up for hours and had not been surprised to see the young priest walk up to his barn. Father Mike could be seen throughout the parish at all hours. This was an odd request but Mr. Wylde asked no questions. He would know soon enough the reason. There were no secrets in Kells."

"I remember Maggie giving a small wave to us as we stood in the front yard. She sat twisted on the wooden bench seat beside Danny looking backwards. Her cheeks were wet and the fingers of her right hand holding tightly to the cross on the chain around her neck," said Bridget reaching up to finger a cross at her own neck. "She stayed that way, with the wagon bouncing along the rutted dirt road until they were over the small hill by the Murray farm and we could no longer see them."

"How awful it must have been for all of you, for her parents," said Ian thinking of his own children.

Danny patted Bridget's knee. "Father Mike had it all worked out for us. We would board a boat in Dublin to Shannon then on to London. I had letters for the captain and Father Mike's Aunt Agatha."

"That was the last time I saw Maggie," said Bridget, as she wiped away tears.

"I stayed with her through that harrowing trip. On the boat to Shannon she had been throwing up and feverish. I knew it was the awful thing that had happened to her, leaving her family, the midnight trip to Dublin, the wretched boat and the frightening weather. No wonder she was ill. But Maggie was a strong girl. Once we got to London I knew she would be alright. I prayed that Aunt Agatha was as kind as Father Mike said."

The six of them sat unmoving and speechless having learned about a secret part of Maggie's life. Lizzie was the first to ask, "Why didn't you tell her he wasn't dead?"

Danny looked at her solemnly, "That night we thought he was going to die. For some time we thought he would. He lost a lot of blood and the rusty spike caused an infection. Several weeks later, thinking he was slowly dying, Last Rites were performed. Brendan made his confession to Father Mike who encouraged him to tell his brother the truth. Fearing for his soul, he did. He told Liam what he had done to Maggie. But then, he didn't die. By the time he was better the town knew the truth and it would have been safe for Maggie to come home."

"We had gotten two letters from her," said Bridget. "She told us what life was like in London. Then nothing. We were never able to find her."

"Did you try? Did you go to London, did you call?" asked Kevin, the questions coming out in a rush.

"The war was on, remember. Mail was not reliable and people didn't have phones like today," Danny said shaking his head. "Things were different."

"I still have the letters, back home, if you would like to see them," said Bridget turning to Lizzie.

"Do you remember what she said in them?" asked Rose.

"Ah, yes I do. I read those letters so many times over the years. She said London was loud. Unceasing noise. Night and day, day and night. Maggie missed the natural quiet of home, the flapping of a blackbird's wing as it takes off from the apple tree in the back yard or the soft whisper of the misting rain on the flowers our mother had planted in pots by the front door. Each day she awoke startled to be somewhere other than the warm soft bed we shared. She expected to hear the murmur of Momma's voice as she talked softly to the twins. Or, hear Da out back in his work shop tapping on the sole of a neighbors leather boot.

"Instead she found herself sharing a bed with Abby a young girl from another town in Ireland. The small room, painted the color of weak tea had one window covered in a lacey curtain. One fat wooden chest trimmed in leather and brass with massive ball feet sat at the foot of each bed and held most the girl's belongings. What wasn't in the chest hung on two black metal hooks on the wall behind the door. A picture of the Blessed Mother in a simple wooden frame hung above the rickety brass bed with peeling white paint. It was a tidy room, ample enough for the two young girls. And, it was across the hall from Aunt Agatha. Maggie said she kept that room for the newest girls in case they needed extra attention. She was a kind, caring woman. I imagine most were so homesick they cried themselves to sleep for the first week or two."

Bridget had been sitting with one hand in her lap and the other firmly held by Danny. She looked up at him and sighed slightly. He patted her hand and continued the story.

"You see, Aunt Agatha was running a boarding house for the young Irish girls working in the shoe factory. Her husband, John, had died in a boating accident shortly after they were married. So for at least ten years Agatha Charles had to take care of herself and in doing so she helped many a young Irish girl make her way in the world. Each of the six girls paid a small portion of their weekly wages to Aunt Agatha for the room and helped her tend to the house after work. None of the girls cared a wit. They were happy to have something to occupy their time and their minds. The four other girls, I believe their names were Mary, Kathleen, Anne and maybe Fiona shared the large attic room. She was settling in, getting to know the others and started to work two weeks after she arrived. The job was not hard. Maggie knew shoes.

"We received her first letter four weeks after she had

arrived in London By then we thought Brendan might still die. He ran a high fever on and off. No antibiotics like today. We had to rely on the local doctor who was a bit of a drunk and there was that woman in Navin who folks said dealt with the little people, the leprechauns. She put together a poultice the smelled like the devil but over time seemed to help. He did live after all."

Bridget added "It might have been another six or eight weeks when we knew for sure he would live and Maggie could come home. We wrote to Aunt Agatha but didn't receive a response."

His brow wrinkled and his lips turned down. Danny explained, "Finally, Father Mike received a letter from the priest in Aunt Agatha's parish. We were told her home had been destroyed by a German bomb. Everyone was dead. The bodies of six girls and middle age woman were found in the rubble."

Chapter 34

Looking directly at Bridget, Lizzie said, "All these years she and Daddy thought she had killed a man. It explains so much. No photos, no talk of family in Ireland, and then the stories she told Dan and I. She lost the present but remembered the past. It come back to haunt her these last few months." Turning to her brothers she said, "I didn't tell you because we didn't know if it was real or not. I thought she might mention something to you but she never did, did she?"

Kevin and Ian both shook their heads. "I don't know if she tried. I kept her in the here and now," said Ian. "I talked about today not the past. Whenever she brought up anything about Ireland or England I would change the subject."

"Me too. I guess I didn't know how to deal with it when she got the least bit emotional. So I pretended I didn't hear," said Kevin shrugging his shoulders as the color rose in his cheeks.

"If only they had tried to contact you," said Lizzie sighing. "How different things would be."

Danny declared, "We all missed out on so much because we didn't know. Because of secrets. We can sit here and talk about what ifs, but it won't bring back the time we lost, the people we lost. What we can do, is get to know our new family and let you get to know us and the family in Ireland."

With that he stood and helped Bridget to her feet. Turning to look at Maggie's three children, a smile on his lips and a twinkle in his eyes he said, "Why don't you introduce us to all of our grandnieces and grandnephews?"

Made in the USA
Monee, IL
17 January 2020